GALLERY
OF
LIES

Ms Ruby,
Thanks so much for supporting this dream of mine. You've always been a voice of positivity and encouragement and helped me to keep pushing until it was finished.

With much love and appreciation,
xo
Jalah Howard
aka Jacinta
11-4-2019

GALLERY OF LIES

Lolah Howard

Empress Lolah
PUBLISHING

EMPRESS LOLAH PUBLISHING
LITHONIA, GA

Copyright © 2019 Jacinta Howard

All rights reserved.

No part of this publication may be reproduced, distributed, or transmitted in any form or by any means, including photocopying, recording, or other electronic or mechanical methods without the prior written permission of the publisher, except in the case of critical reviews and certain other noncommercial uses permitted by copyright law.

Published in the United States by Empress Lolah Publishing, LLC.

Gallery of Lies is a work of fiction. Names, characters, places, and incidents either are the product of the author's imagination or are used fictitiously. Any resemblance to actual persons, living or dead, events, or locals is entirely coincidental.

Visit author Lolah Howard's website at:

http://www.lolahhoward.com

eISBN: 978-1-7333569-0-3

Print ISBN: 978-1-7333596-1-0

Cover design by Damonza.

Edited by Kirsten Jennings

Contents

CHAPTER 1 1

CHAPTER 2 5

CHAPTER 3 13

CHAPTER 4 19

CHAPTER 5 25

CHAPTER 6 31

CHAPTER 7 37

CHAPTER 8 41

CHAPTER 9 49

CHAPTER 10 55

CHAPTER 11 59

CHAPTER 12 65

CHAPTER 13 71

CHAPTER 14 77

CHAPTER 15 87

CHAPTER 16 91

CHAPTER 17 93

CHAPTER 18 101

CHAPTER 19 109

CHAPTER 20 115

CHAPTER 21	121
CHAPTER 22	125
CHAPTER 23	129
CHAPTER 24	133
CHAPTER 25	139
CHAPTER 26	143
CHAPTER 27	147
CHAPTER 28	151
CHAPTER 29	157
CHAPTER 30	161
CHAPTER 31	169
CHAPTER 32	175
CHAPTER 33	181
CHAPTER 34	187
CHAPTER 35	191
CHAPTER 36	197
CHAPTER 37	203
CHAPTER 38	207
CHAPTER 39	213
CHAPTER 40	217
ABOUT THE AUTHOR	223

For everyone that listened to me talk about this book for years and the little critique group that helped me get through.

CHAPTER 1

THERE ARE SOME THINGS inherently disappointing about being married that nobody mentions before you do it. One of them was just how selfish people could be even though they're supposed to be your partner. I sat there looking at a selfish ass as he bent down in front of the dryer. He reached in and felt to see if his socks and underwear were dry. While he bent over, I was tempted to run up behind him and shove him in. To keep myself from doing something irrational, I walked into our bedroom and plopped on the bed. My tablet rested on the bedside table, and I picked it up. I opened Facebook and scrolled through my "friends" pictures of their babies, cute kids, and dogs doing adorable and obnoxious things. I hoped that on the outside I was the picture of calm iciness as Mike walked back into our bedroom and pressed the folded underwear and socks into his suitcase that rested on the floor at the foot of the bed. I refused to look up at him even as I knew he was looking at me.

"Mona, do we have any bars of soap?"

I didn't look up, "I don't know, I don't use bars of soap, I use body wash. Look in the cabinet."

He smacked his lips. He wanted me to react, but I wasn't going to because that would mean that I cared. There was soap in the bathroom, but I was not going to help him. Let him find it himself.

He yelled from the bathroom. "Which cabinet Mona?"

"I don't remember."

My finger was scrolling furiously over the screen. I immediately stopped. I heard cabinets opening and closing. Yes, it was passive aggressive of me.

Oh well. He walked out of the bathroom holding two bars of Irish Spring up in the air like he had won a trophy.

"I found it."

I looked up and then back down at the tablet. One of my friends had gone back to her maiden name. That was a trend on Facebook amongst friends from high school. A lot of the folks that got married around the same time I did were back to being a party of one. Well, hell, I'm a party of one, and I'm still married so I couldn't say anything.

He stood there over his suitcase in his NC State basketball shorts and a black tank top looking like he was about to go to a three point shootout with the exception that his tan feet were bare.

"Mona, so are you just going to give me the silent treatment all night before I leave? You know I hate leaving out on bad terms."

"I'm not giving you the silent treatment. I'm just quiet. Can't I be quiet sometimes?"

He looked at me and crooked his lips up to one side, showing me his skepticism. I twisted my lips right back at him.

"Come on baby. I know that I told you I'd be back in time to go with you to your conference, but that was before I found out they had given me back to back assignments. There's no need for me to come back to Atlanta when I leave Washington and then turn and fly to Phoenix the next day."

I tried to remain silent, Lord knows I tried, but I just could not let this pass.

"Mike, you know that this is not the issue. You have promised me that you will stop traveling so much and now here you are staying gone even longer than usual. What is it so great out there that you won't stay home? I am so sick of having this conversation with you."

His brown eyes rolled up to the ceiling, and he let out a sigh that pushed my level of pissed up a notch. Like I wasn't an understanding wife. I had understood for six years of this bull.

"Mona, I have interviewed for four different positions, and I haven't gotten them. What do you think I am supposed to do? I am not going to take a pay cut or go back to being a driver."

"All I keep hearing is what you're not going to do. I'm going to start telling you what I'm not going to do. I'm not going to listen to you stand here acting like you have been trying so hard to stay local. I'm not going to act like I am okay with this."

I hopped up off the bed walked over to my dresser and snatched open a drawer. I pulled out a pair of sweats to wear to bed. Mike glanced down at them and sighed again. He knew that sweats meant he wasn't getting none of THIS tonight. There was no need for him to attempt to snuggle up with me or anything else that crossed his mind. Let him suffer. He walked back to the laundry room and came back with some more clothes neatly folded and put them in the bag. I went into the bathroom, closed the door, and changed out of my slacks and shirt into sweats and a t-shirt. For extra measure, I pulled my straightened hair up, wrapped it around my head, opened a drawer, pulled out a silk scarf, and tied it up like Aunt Jemima. I usually only dressed like this when he was gone. He could disappoint me, so tonight he would be disappointed too.

When I walked back into the bedroom, the TV glowed, and he was already under the covers. I got in the bed as far away from him as I could get on a king-sized mattress. Again, I picked up my tablet and scrolled through more of my friend's posts to see how many more of them had gotten smart and dropped their hyphenated names along with their husbands. Mike kept glancing over at me. I knew what he wanted more than just some sex for the road. He wanted to get me pregnant, and sweatpants were a definite form of birth control.

"Mona, can we talk calmly? Look I don't want to go to bed mad tonight."

"Why don't you care about leaving me? Just be honest, are you trying to get away from me? Or is it just something better out there on the road?"

"Look, Mona, you know there's nobody. You know I would never do that to you."

I didn't know anything. You can't put anything past anyone. The sad thing was that I don't know if I would even care if Mike had another woman if he brought his ass home. He could have a local chick... I was not about to tell him that though.

"I never thought you would leave me alone like this all the time, but you do. You can quit that job. I make enough at Wells Fargo to float us, we have savings."

"We have discussed this; you know I am not going to do that. I'm not the kind of man to quit a job and let my wife work."

There it was again, what he was not going to do...

"Yeah, but aren't we supposed to be a team. I know you're not a bum."

He stood there shaking his head as I talked.

"You know what... It doesn't even matter," I said.

He reached for me, but I pushed him away. I turned my back to him and didn't say anything else. I was tired of giving him passes and being understanding and waiting for him to make a change. I was tired of being disappointed. I was tired of living like a single woman and going to events solo. I was tired of being alone all the time. That was why people got married wasn't it, so that they had a companion? I felt like I had lost my best friend a long time ago because that is what he used to be, my best friend. I wanted to soften for him, but it would just hurt more when he left tomorrow morning. Yes, it would hurt that he was going, but it hurt so much worse to know that I wasn't important enough for him to stay.

He turned the TV off, and I lay there motionless. We both breathed into the silence for what had to be half an hour before I felt him move and put his thigh against mine. There was no point in kicking him off. I might as well relax and go to sleep. There would be many sleepless nights for the next month while he was gone. Might as well enjoy it while I could.

CHAPTER 2

I PULLED UP IN the parking lot outside of the Wing Café on Camp Creek Parkway. There was an empty spot next to Cheryl's SUV. She put on red lipstick while looking up into her visor mirror. Red was her party lipstick shade, and she always wore it when we went out. I never wore red, and I wondered how it would look on me. She looked over and did a little wave. I opened my door, and she stepped out of her car also.

I scoped out the inside of the bar.

"Girl this place is pretty packed for a Thursday. I hope this isn't a young crowd."

She smiled as if this was a good thing. "Yeah it is crowded, but from what I heard, this is always like this, and it is folks our age. I just wanted to try something different, and as I told you, the word is they have a great karaoke DJ. You know we gotta do our song."

Cheryl reached and tugged her short dress down as she said this. She had ditched the suit from work and in its place were a cute little blue flirty knit dress and high-heeled sandals. I had opted for tight ripped jeans and tall wedges with an earth tone off-shoulder peasant top. I was channeling the seventies, with my afro pushed back from my forehead tied with a colorful scarf. We walked towards the door, and I noticed the row of motorcycles lined up in front of the building. It appeared that this was the hot spot for bikers. Some eye candy would be good. Anything to get my mind off the argument that I'd had with Mike before he left. I might as well do some karaoke and try to enjoy myself. I had wanted to tell Cheryl about it at work today, but then again I was just so tired of discussing my relationship. I was tired of complaining about the same thing repeatedly. In the end, didn't that make me look like the dummy in this situation, complaining about something that never changed?

We walked into the place, and it held way more bodies than expected. I looked around and only saw two empty tables in the whole place. One table had only one chair while the one over near the corner of the bar had two. Cheryl immediately made a beeline for the table with two chairs and sat down. I followed her and saw that two other women had been walking towards the table. We had lucked out; there was no way I had wanted to stand all night. Cheryl said as much.

"Girl it looks like we were just in time. They were moving too slow."

I giggled. "Don't get us beat up in here hijacking tables."

She pursed her lips and looked at me. "Who are they going to beat up? I have you here to protect me. They aren't going to mess with your Amazon ass up in here. In those wedges, you are about seven feet tall."

At this comment, she laughed loudly at her own joke. I gave her the side eye. A server walked up to our table and put two menus down with two glasses of water. She introduced herself as Bebe as she swung her blond butt length braids over her shoulder.

"Do y'all need a minute to look at the menu or do you know what you want already?" Bebe displayed her perfectly sculpted abs and pierced belly button with her white t-shirt tied in a knot. She smiled at us expectantly while her hand rested on a slim hip covered in bleached denim. I bet she earned lots of tips with this crowd.

I spoke up. "I know I want a long Island right now. By the time you come back, I will know what I want to eat."

Cheryl raised an eyebrow at my order. "Well Bebe, it looks like she is going for it. I will have a margarita on the rocks with salt on the rim."

Bebe nodded, "Yeah honey, the bartender pours heavy on those Long Islands." With that, she sashayed away.

Cheryl turned to me. "Umm ... you are going hard for a Thursday aren't you? What's up?"

I shook my head. "Nothing, I just have a taste for a Long Island. Besides, if you want to do this karaoke thing, I need a little courage to sing in front of this crowd. This audience isn't like the one at that little Honky Tonk place we go to with the coworkers. These folks might send the Sandman out if we bomb."

Cheryl apparently thought I was making a joke since she laughed. I was serious. Our table was over on the far right wall near the door that led out to a patio that held a crowd of people. It looked to be where most of the bikers were sitting since I saw numerous guys wearing motorcycle vests. In the middle of the place was a massive three-sided bar and on the other side were more tables and booths near a sign that indicated the bathroom. The DJ was on that side too with a tiny stage that held a microphone stand and a big screen used to display the words to the songs. I saw several people with thick spiral notebooks, flipping through the pages looking for their musical selections.

When Bebe came back to the table, Cheryl and I ordered some Buffalo wings and tater tots. I planned to have several drinks and the greasy food would help me to avoid getting sick by drinking alcohol on an empty stomach. Bebe had already put in the order for my second drink. Cheryl raised an eyebrow but didn't say anything this time. The song that had been playing over the loudspeaker stopped, and the DJ introduced the next person to sing. I couldn't see the stage that well from where we were sitting, but when the girl started singing she had a beautiful voice belting out a Whitney Houston song. These weren't amateurs. I was beginning to change my mind about singing. I had a decent voice, but it was kind of deep and raspy, not like this damn songbird up there now. She had everyone singing along in her Whitney tribute.

When the song was over, the DJ introduced another person. This time a chubby, balding guy did a rap song. He didn't get all of the words right, but he made up for it in enthusiasm as everybody started standing up and rapping along with him. I felt a little better; maybe it was more about crowd involvement. Leaning over to the table next to me, I asked a woman if I could see the book when she finished. She passed it to me just as Bebe brought our food.

"Cheryl, what song are we going to sing? Now we need to get this together," I said.

She laughed at me. She knew I was an overachiever.

"I don't know, let's do the usual."

"I don't want to sing that for this crowd," I said.

"Well pick something, what about an Erykah Badu song? That one would be good with your voice."

I flipped through the book. "That's a good idea."

There were plenty of her songs in the catalog. I chose one and wrote it on the slip of paper that was on the table. Cheryl walked over to the DJ booth while I finished off my first drink and started on the second one. Out of the corner of my eye, I saw a figure brush past our table coming from the patio door. By the time I glanced up, all I could see was the back of his biker jacket with the letters 'JD' and the word 'Picasso' embossed along with the club name 'Street Kingz' as he walked across the club towards the bathrooms. He was tall, at least 6'8" or 6'9" by the way he towered over everyone else. My eyes followed him across the room as I tried to catch a glimpse of his face, but he never turned around. Cheryl made her way back and sat down.

"When the DJ comes back from his break, there are two more singers then we are up."

I groaned and slurped at my drink. A hip-hop song came over the loudspeakers, and the DJ came from behind his turntables and headed over to talk to the bartender. We both bobbed our head to the music as we finished nibbling on our wings. When Bebe came back by, Cheryl ordered another margarita, and I ordered drink number three.

Cheryl turned to me. "So how's everything going? We haven't seen you and Mike lately; it's time for another game night isn't it?"

"It's going... Sure, we can have a game night. If Mike comes home anytime soon, I will let him know."

Cheryl's smile left her lips. "Why did you say 'if' he comes home? Girl, what's up? Is everything good with y'all?"

I nodded. "It's fine. I'm just talking. I think he's supposed to be back next week. It's been a long trip this time, that's all."

She nodded slowly. "Yeah, I know it's hard. But maybe you need to have another talk about it."

What she didn't know was that I was so sick of him, but then again, maybe she did. She had been the one to listen to me rant about this for the past who knows how many years. I was leaving here and going to an empty house; she wasn't. Was that a little resentment bubbling up to the surface? This wasn't the time or place to discuss this. I didn't want to get angry or sad tonight. Just then, the sound of our names being called over the speakers saved me from this discussion. I instantly downed the last of my drink before I stood up.

Gallery of Lies

Cheryl led the way to the stage, and as I walked, I felt the alcohol from those drinks rushing to my head, but I felt pretty damned good. We were going to get this crowd swaying.

The music started, and I saw some heads bobbing throughout the room. We both swayed our hips to the melody. I giggled a little at how we must have looked on stage, Cheryl, light skinned and only 5'1" compared to my dark complexion standing at over six feet in these wedges. We were Ebony and Ivory. I think I laughed out loud at my thought. I bobbed my head and moved to the music as Cheryl started the song in her high clear voice. She was a good singer. People clapped as she hit a high note. I joined in with her on the chorus, and I saw some people joining in singing the bridge. Some ladies stood up and started moving their hands back and forth in the air as they sang along. Then I started singing my verse.

I closed my eyes, and my low voice filled the room. I heard applause, and my eyes popped open. That's when I saw him standing back near the bathrooms. It looked as if he was looking right into my eyes. I sang and moved my arm to the rhythm while my hips shimmied to the drum line. I loved to dance. It looked like he was watching me. I supposed everyone was. I reached down and brought a low growling note up from my chest. I don't know if it sounded good, but people started clapping and yelling for us as Cheryl's and my voices joined in harmony. When the song ended, we got a standing ovation, and we both bowed as if this was the Apollo. When we walked off stage, women were giving us high fives. My eyes met his again, he hadn't moved, but he was concentrating on my face. Cheryl laughed and hugged me.

"Girl that was so good. Where did that growl come from? I have never heard you get into it like that."

I swiped my hand across my forehead and felt sweat there. "It was those Long Islands. Now they are making me hot. Let me go to the ladies room."

She nodded and made headed back towards the table. I turned back towards where he had been standing, but he was gone. I went into the bathroom and splashed a little cold water on my face. I drank those cocktails too fast. I knew better. I dried my face and hands and headed out. He was standing there in the short hallway by the door of the men's room. I should have been surprised, but I wasn't. He pressed himself against the wall as if to allow me to squeeze past him. I moved slowly by him as I let my eyes rest on his face.

9

Just as I brushed past him, his hand snaked out and grasped my wrist softly. I halted and turned towards him. He was so tall that I had to hold my head back to look up into his eyes, which didn't happen to me often. He didn't smile and neither did I. A mustache and goatee framed full lips that he licked before he gave me that intense look that men give you when they are sexually interested. This man was accustomed to getting what he wanted whenever he wanted it.

When his lips moved the sound that came out was a deep rumble that vibrated some string in me that no one had strummed in a long time.

He said, "I was hoping to catch you back here before you got back to your seat."

I said from under my lashes, "Oh, yeah, what for?"

He smiled finally, "I think you know. You were doing something to me when you were up on that stage. You were looking at me when you were singing, weren't you? I thought you wanted to talk to me like I wanted to talk to you. But, I didn't know if you wanted your friend to know."

He pulled my left hand up between us and kissed the back of it. Then he held it up between us and let his thumb rest on the solitary stone set on the ring finger of my left hand and looked deep into my eyes. I pulled my hand away from him. For a split second, I thought he would have something smart to say, or make some joke. I didn't know that he had already seen the ring, not that I was trying to hide it. He pulled his cell phone from his pocket.

"Put your phone number in here and let me know when it's cool to contact you."

At that moment, I felt powerful and sexy. I was in control of this situation. I held the phone in my hand and stared at the colorful background image of paint splatters he had on his screen. I knew that giving him my number would open a black hole. I started to enter the numbers and then at the last minute I changed my mind. I handed the phone back to him and backed up.

"No, it's not what you think. I was just feeling the music."

He smiled as he took the phone back. "That's alright baby. I understand. You're not ready for this, but you are looking for something. You just don't know it yet. I hope I see you around, and I'm there when you figure it out."

He then turned and walked into the men's restroom. I stood there speechless for a second. His arrogance upset me and at the same time made me feel invigorated. He was so cocky and opposite of the type of man I usually dealt with.

I walked back to my table, and the server came over to me to see if I wanted anything else from the bar. I ordered a refill on my water and told her to bring the tab. Cheryl chattered on about how much fun karaoke was. She said we needed to come back to this spot soon. What she didn't know was that I would not be joining her. I had almost given that man my phone number, and in the back of my mind, I was still thinking how I wish I had. Yes, Cheryl could come back up here all by herself. I had just discovered just how dangerous of a place this actually was.

CHAPTER 3

I SLAMMED MY HAND down on the alarm clock and heard something hit the floor with a thud. I hoped it wasn't the bottle of baby oil I always forgot re-cap after I used it, one of Mike's pet peeves. I sat up in bed and looked down at myself. Why was I wearing a shirt instead of my gown? Then his face flashed into my memory. It was the man from last night that I'd almost given my phone number too. I threw an arm over my eyes at the disturbing memories and what felt like the beginning pangs of a headache.

I knew better than to drink that much. I flipped the cover back to see that at least I'd had the sense to take off my jeans and shoes. The little scarf that had been holding my afro back lay crumpled on the sheet beside me in the bed. I had forgotten to wrap my hair up, and it was probably springing out in every direction on top of my head. This was not going to be a good morning. I had at least eight more minutes before the alarm chimed again, so I pulled the cover back up over my head, but my mind was racing too much to go back to sleep.

I was shocked at myself for even entertaining the idea of talking to another man. I could picture him standing there nodding along as we sang, looking all tall and rich chocolate like a Mr. Goodbar. I groaned. I was horny. That's what my problem was. I had been angry and horny. Wasn't that always a dangerous combination? I got up and opened the cabinet under the sink to find some ibuprofen. After choking back two pills, I put my mouth under the tap for a gulp of water. Mike needed to come home soon. However, until then, when I got back from work tonight I would need to do a little something special on our video call to keep me from losing my mind.

***

I clicked off the call with Mike. Skype hadn't been working. The Holiday Inn Express he was in had a slow Wi-Fi connection. It was frustrating, being in a long distance relationship with my husband. I had been feeling sexy and maybe even a little naughty. I intended to engage in a bit of video call sex. The slow connection had killed my vibe, and we ended up just talking the regular old way. I cut the conversation short in my annoyance. After some time thinking about things, the carpet had started to show a groove from my pacing. A glance at the clock and I realized it was just a little before eight o'clock and way too early to go to sleep. There were plenty of clothes I could fold, so I stepped into the laundry room. I turned the light on, looked at the pile of clean laundry, and turned the light back off. Folding clothes wasn't what I wanted to do tonight.

I looked over at the stairs that lead to the third floor. I took them up to the top, opened the door, and flipped on the light. It had been a weeks since I had been up here. The walls were a buttery yellow that I had painted myself when I had claimed this attic as my craft room. Built-in shelving and work tables surrounded the area. A big window faced out to the front of the house looking down over our quiet street. In the daytime, the space filled with beautiful bright sunlight that was perfect for painting. In the middle sat my easel. On it was a half done rendering of purple daisies. On a waist-high stool next to the easel rested a yellow vase with a clump of brown dried flowers drooping towards the floor. I laughed to myself. The flowers looked like I felt. I picked up the vase and dumped the flowers into the wastebasket in the corner.

Gallery of Lies

A stack of blank canvases rested on the worktable on the left. I picked up the abandoned painting of purple flowers and grabbed a new blank canvas with which to replace it. I got my paints and brushes off a shelf and put them on the small table next to my easel. Then I took the two empty jars from the shelf and headed back down the laundry room sink to fill them with water for my brushes. When I got down there, I dashed down one more level and grabbed a bottle of merlot out of the wine rack in the kitchen and a glass before heading back upstairs. With my jars filled and my glass full of wine, I sat on the stool and stared at the blank canvas. What was I going to paint? The wine bottle caught my attention, and I decided that would be my subject.

First, I primed my canvas with three coats of the white Gesso from its plastic tub so that it could air dry. Then I picked up the palette and squeezed out blobs of black, white, blue, red, and yellow paints. I selected a medium sized brush and started to swirl the paints to mix and create new colors. I put the brush to canvas and started painting. It felt good to create something with my hands and see the image start to take form as I filled in the background with abstract shading. Then I outlined the bottle, and the picture began to take shape. It didn't matter to me how it looked. I wasn't an extraordinary painter, but my mind got lost in my creation. I felt my frustration with failed phone sex melt away. I picked up the glass of wine, drank it down, and moved over to the old radio in the corner. My fingers turned the dial and tuned the radio to the jazz station.

A saxophone refrain with soulful elements came through the tiny speakers. I sat back on the stool in front of my creation. My hands flew over the canvas. Paint stained my shirt while my forgotten smock lay on the floor, but I didn't care. The dark color was under my nails and on my forearms. My feelings of disappointment dripped out through the brush strokes as I swirled and dabbed the paint onto the canvas. The DJ at the radio station told us all listening to enjoy the quiet storm. This was love making music. Tonight this canvas was my lover, attuned to my moods, and taking on all of my emotions. I thought back to the first art class that I took in college. I loved doing anything with my hands from pottery spinning to jewelry making. I tried them all, but they didn't soothe my soul like painting.

I remembered when Mike and I went Sips and Strokes with Cheryl and Ray three summers ago. Mike was on vacation for two weeks. Cheryl found the deal on Groupon for four people to take a two-hour painting class. It was BYOB, bring your own bottle. Cheryl showed up at the house with a huge picnic basket, and we had made sandwiches and fried chicken wings to take with us. I added two bottles of wine to the basket. Not surprisingly, for all of our enthusiasm, the guys weren't so excited about our activity selection. Not many men wanted to be dragged to a painting class, but we knew that in spite of their reservations it would be fun.

We arrived at the class to find it packed with other couples like us as well as groups of women that looked like they were enjoying a girls' night out. Everyone found their spaces and set out their selection of food and different bottles of alcohol of all type. The guys' attitudes changed a little when we got there, and they found that we had packed bottles of Heineken in the basket. As the evening continued on, we had all started to have a good time. We got tipsy, and while Cheryl and I followed along with the wispy blond instructor to paint pictures of high-heeled shoes, the guys chose to paint the Atlanta Falcons logo. We ate the sandwiches and wings that we had packed, the grease on our fingers mixing with the different colors of paint. Bouts of laughter and giggles broke out all over the studio, as the others in the class seemed to be feeling their drinks as well. Mike kissed me sweetly as I spread the paint on the canvas with no accuracy. I looked over, and Ray had his arm around Cheryl's waist as she smiled up into his face. Our paintings were amateurish at best. Neither of them would ever hang over my mantle, but they were relics of what now seemed like a rare night of fun. If I looked in the closet, those canvases lie there disregarded somewhere in the dark, cluttered space.

I hadn't thought of that night in a long time. I remember coming home, dropping the paintings in the foyer and pulling at each other's clothes. We never made it to the bed, but made love on the sofa in front of the fireplace. The change in the DJ's voice on the radio to a female's sexy tone tugged me from my reverie. She announced that she was Joyce Chavelle coming on for the midnight love.

I opened and closed my hands and stretched the fatigue out of my fingers as I put the brush down. Time had sped along while thoughts of the past occupied my mind. The lateness of the hour on the clock surprised me. I sat back and looked at my painting that felt too flat and lifeless. It was full of somber strokes of black and brown. There streaked tones of Merlot that matched the small amount of liquid left in my glass. The rendering of the wine bottle was mediocre, but my mood had improved from the melancholy state I had been in earlier. I needed to think of the good times more often since, lately, I had been wallowing in the bad emotions surrounding my marriage.

    Tomorrow, I was going to get on my computer and find an art class in the city that would allow me to improve my painting skills. Exactly, that's what I needed, something to bring back the passions that I used to enjoy. I could fill my nights with good memories and create works of art instead of dwelling on how lonely I felt

CHAPTER 4

MY GPS INFORMED ME that I had arrived though there was no signage outside, just shiny numbers stuck to the glass door. I opened the door and walked in even though I was still unsure if I was in the right place. The interior looked like an abandoned office building down to the imitation Berber carpet squares. It was apparent that the previous owners of the building had abandoned the forlorn receptionist's desk years ago, but taped to the front of it was a computer printed sign that read 'The Master's Studio'.

I was in the right location even though it looked nothing like I had envisioned an artist's studio would. I walked past it and headed down a hallway. Along the hall were several rooms that must have been offices in a previous life. At the end of the corridor, stood double doors labeled 'The Master's Studio'.

I walked through the doors and immediately could tell that this had been the assembly room for this office building. To the left of me was a table laid out with bottled water and coffee and its fixings. A tall blonde man and a short redhead stood near the coffee stirring the liquid in their cups. They looked up, and I smiled at them and spoke a hello. To the right was the front of the room where a small stage was set up with an easel, stool, and paint supplies. In front of the stage, sat two rows of easels spread out.

On the front row but to the far left, one easel stood unclaimed. As I put my bag on the stool, two women walked in together. The older woman had waist length salt and pepper gray dreadlocks, and the younger woman sported an auburn afro, but in their faces was an uncanny resemblance that had to be that of a mother-daughter pair. They said hellos as they walked in, and I spoke back and smiled. I was getting excited to meet the instructor. I had read reviews of this class, and this instructor received mostly four-star ratings.

I reached into my bag and started digging around for my phone to make sure that I silenced it before the class began. I responded to a text from Cheryl and then looked at the time. This instructor had better not be late. I heard the door open and close again behind me and looked up to see the man I had talked to in the wing cafe striding up the aisle towards the front of the class. What the hell? This man didn't look like the type that would be taking an art class, but I guess that was stereotyping. He walked up and stood in front of the stage, evidently looking for a spot. I tried to shrink down behind my easel while he stood there. It looked like he was counting or maybe he was just trying to find two easels together. I was hoping that one of the other people that were in the class would hurry and claim the easel next to mine before he chose it for himself.

I knew I was too damn tall to try to hide, especially with my hair in a wild afro that added at least four inches to my height, but I still stooped down and attempted to go unnoticed. *Please don't choose the easel next to me.* Then I realized my arrogance in this situation. What made me think this man would remember me with all of the women he most likely talked to on a daily basis? I stood up straight. Why was I hiding? He could be taking this class with his girlfriend, wife, or something. When homeboy stepped up onto the stage and put his messenger bag on a table, I was confused and then stunned. He then took off the motorcycle jacket that I remembered and laid it on the table too before glancing down at his watch and turning towards the classroom with a sheet of paper in his hand. Now the word 'Picasso' on the back of his jacket made sense.

"Good evening everyone if I can get your attention. My name is Jason Derrick Terry. Please call me JD, and I want to welcome you to The Master's Studio painting series. This one is all about creating movement in your paintings. We have a small class this week; there will only be eight of you. I see there are six of you here. Hopefully, the other two will be coming along soon."

He proceeded to tell us about his background. He had attended the well-renowned SCAD, Savannah College of Art and Design, and become an illustrator and graphic artist. I was entirely wrong on my first impression of this dude. He paced slowly around the stage as he talked. The sleeves of his gray henley shirt were folded up to his elbows. The soft cotton molded to his shoulders as if it had been washed hundreds of times. Splotches of old paint decorated the front of his jeans and splattered boots covered his feet.

One other person entered the class while he talked. He looked down at the sheet of paper and started to call out names as people raised their hands he checked them off with a pen. He called my name, and I didn't say anything. I glanced at the exit door, but then I thought of the money I'd paid to take this class. It probably wasn't refundable. What was my reason for asking for a refund? The teacher is just too damn fine. He called my name again.

"So Mona isn't here yet?"

I cleared my throat and raised my hand. He looked over at me and went to put a check mark on the paper when his head snapped back up, and he met my eyes. A smirk briefly touched his lips before he dropped his gaze and called the next name. Did he recognize me? As I contemplated the rationale of trying to sneak out quietly, he walked over to a table at the far right of the stage and picked up a canvas that had been resting there. On it was a painting of two horses galloping across a field and began to speak. Dammit, leaving now would look strange.

Maybe I imagined the smirk. I could tough it out through the end of the class. He gave us an overview of what he would be teaching as he put his paints on a palette. We all followed along, watching his efficient movements. He talked, and my eyes kept going back to the cords in his forearms as he moved the brush over the canvas. His hands were big; the fingernails cut short and blunt. His hands looked strong and capable while the way that he moved them had a grace that I normally would not have associated with a man so overtly masculine. His back was to us, the students, as he became the master that his bio had proclaimed. He explained brush technique in a way that I had never heard before. He made it simple. I focused on his back, the muscles bunching and stretching as he gestured with the brush in his hand. I forced myself to look down at my canvas and try to replicate, with much less than perfection, the painting that he created right before our eyes.

At the end of the two-hour session, he told us to take our supplies but leave our labeled canvases to dry. I picked up my palette and brushes and went to one four deep sinks to rinse my tools. The two women that I noticed earlier lined up behind me to go next. The older woman that I had assumed to be the mother spoke first.

"Tasha, I was surprised when he walked in and said he was the teacher. I didn't expect him to be black. He is a handsome young man, and he didn't have a ring on his finger."

The younger woman made a shushing noise. "Ma, keep your voice down. You are always trying to hook me up. I told you that Steve and I are dating now."

So, I was right about their relationship. Mom smacked her lips.

"Child, Steve is ok, but he is as dry as a piece of toast. Plus you and the master artist would make much prettier grand-babies."

I couldn't help but laugh as I finished and turned away from the sinks. The younger woman smacked her mother on the arm playfully. "See ma. You are acting up."

She looked at me. "Don't mind my mother; she's always trying to embarrass me."

Her mother smiled at me with and leaned in as if she was about to tell me a secret.

"Honey, I see you have a ring on yourself but you ain't dead. I know you had to be looking at him because even I was checking him out with my old self. Look over there and tell me that isn't one fine hunk of chocolate. Reminds me of my husband when we first met."

She pointed across the room at JD talking to one of the other female students. Her daughter grabbed her hand.

"Stop pointing."

I already liked these two. "Yes ma'am, he is a nice looking guy."

She snorted very loudly. "You are darned right. I've been trying to help my Tasha here find a husband for the past two years and she doesn't ever take my advice."

Tasha rolled her eyes. "I have a boyfriend mom."

"Ok, ok. I will let it go, but I think you are missing out on an opportunity. Why don't you just go on over there and ask him some questions."

Tasha walked to the sink and started washing what looked to be both of their tools while her mother stood there with me as if she had no intention of getting off the topic.

"You know what ma; I'm just going to ignore you right now."

Tasha looked as if she was blushing to the tips of her hair. Poor thing, but her mom was hilarious.

"I'm Mona by the way, and it is very nice to meet the both of you."

The woman grabbed my hand for a shake. "Nice to meet you, Mona. I'm Val, and that's my daughter Tasha. We go around doing little classes and things like this to have mother-daughter time together."

I felt a pang of envy that I had not felt in a long time. I would give anything to have my mother here alive to embarrass me.

I made small talk for a little longer and then moved back to my easel to pack my things. I crouched down to reach my bag. When I stood up, JD was standing in front of me.

"So how did you enjoy the class?"

My heartbeat sped up. "Oh, ummm, I enjoyed it a lot. You are a good teacher."

He smiled, and the curve of his lips transformed his expression from that of a professional teacher to the embodiment of sexiness.

"I certainly appreciate that compliment coming from you."

He was standing in my personal space and the cologne he wore filled my senses. Damn, he smelled good. I took a step back, and he chuckled.

"Running into each other again like this has to be a sign of something. Something good I think. I am going to enjoy teaching this class."

He backed away. Before turning around said, "I look forward to seeing you on Thursday night."

I let out a breath I didn't know I was holding. Mr. Art Teacher did remember our first encounter. This class was supposed to be a way to keep my mind occupied with positive thoughts. Somehow, I'd gotten in here with the one distraction I didn't need. Taking this class may not have been such a good idea after all.

CHAPTER 5

THURSDAY AFTERNOON, Cheryl stepped into my office and plopped her narrow behind in my guest chair. I looked up from my perusal of the UPS careers website. I was supposed to be working on a marketing campaign for national accounts, but every now and then I looked to see if there were any open non-travel positions over at UPS that Mike could apply for in Atlanta. There always were. She placed box in front of me from Panera Bread and proceeded to open an identical box on her lap. Evidently somebody had some extra lunches left over from their meeting in the conference room.

"Girl, let me tell you what Ray did yesterday."

She never waited for invitation or acknowledgment, but launched into a release of thoughts and feelings that seemed to come out of nowhere. We had been friends long enough that I knew what to expect. I smiled and indulged her.

"Why is Ray in the doghouse now?"

"Well his ass is going to be the dog's permanent roommate if he doesn't chill out some damn where. I'm in the kitchen last night putting some chicken breasts in the oven when I hear this loud rumble outside. At first I thought it was the neighbors, but then I hear the garage going up. I know this doesn't sound like Ray's car so I rush to the door and yank it open ... Ask me what I see."

I knew this was a rhetorical statement, so I didn't interrupt. She talked on while I took a bite of the turkey sandwich that was in my box.

"I see my dear husband pulling into the garage in a bright yellow Camaro with the black stripes down the middle like that car in that movie... you know what I'm talking about, Bumblebee, from Transformers. We had talked about him getting a new car, but we decided that he needed to get something a little lower in price. I figure that he's driving this car because he's doing a test drive to get me to fall in love with it. You know, so I will agree to keep it."

Cheryl popped up out of the chair and began to pace back and forth on her blue stiletto pumps.

"So I'm just standing there with my hand on my hip, mean mugging him as he gets out of the car. I say, 'Ray what the hell are you doing with that car? You shouldn't have even test driven it, because it's just going to make it that much harder to take it back and choose something else.' He then looks me dead in the eye and says, 'I'm not taking it back.' "

She stopped pacing then and whirled around to look at me finally.

"Girl I couldn't even respond because I just knew this fool didn't say what I think he said. So I said, 'What do you mean you're not taking it back?' He says, 'Just what it sounds like. I'm keeping it'. So I tell him. 'The hell you are, just take it right on back, as a matter of fact I'm going with you and we can take it back right now'."

She starts pacing again with her hands gesturing wildly. If she gets anymore worked up she's going to knock one of my plaques off the shelf behind her. I open my chips and put two in my mouth.

"He then had the nerve to brush past me on into the kitchen like I wasn't even standing there. I followed his behind upstairs, and I'm screaming at him. Needless to say, we argued almost all damn night cause get this... He had already signed the papers and traded his car in! To hell with me and what we had discussed."

With that last statement she plopped back down in the chair, arms crossed and leg bouncing.

I'm shocked to say the least. Ray has never been the type of guy to do anything like this.

I said, "Girl I can't believe he bought it without asking you. Maybe he's having some type of mid-life crisis. I hear these men go through some shit when they start thinking they are getting old."

Cheryl just rolled her eyes and made a rude unlady like noise. "Yeah, that's what I'm worried about. Next thing I know he will be tweeting a picture of his dick to some millennial girl somewhere. I don't think it would bother me so much if it was just a car; it's the fact that he was just so defiant, like he dared me to say something. It's not like we hadn't talked about it. I just don't know, didn't he know this was going to cause a problem with me, with us. Things have already been strained."

I didn't know this. I have always thought of Cheryl and Ray as being the couple that I wanted to be when I grew up.

"Y'all are having problems? I mean, I guess every marriage hits a rough patch... "

I sure was one to talk. Cheryl was my girl but I couldn't tell her what's going on. I wanted to tell somebody, but wasn't that always the way that people got caught, running their mouths too damn much? I listened to her talk about Ray and how they barely had sex anymore and how everything was so boring. I wished my husband was at home for me to get bored with. Most of the time, I didn't even feel like I was married anymore.

Suddenly Cheryl deflated like a discarded birthday balloon. Her hand went up to her face, and she sucked in her lips and wiped her fingers across her mouth.

"I'm scared Mona," she said without meeting my eyes.

This was more serious than I thought. Cheryl lost her bravado and attitude. I saw the fear in her face. I didn't say anything because I didn't know what was appropriate. She looked down at her left hand on her lap and then finally up at me.

"I'm not sure this is just a rough patch this time. It's not the same, I mean we've had our ups and downs, but it's different this time. Things don't feel the same between us."

I was so stunned to hear this. Cheryl always acted like everything was gravy between them. Their relationship was always different from everyone else's anyway. They always argued; well let me rephrase that, Cheryl always fussed at Ray and he humored her. But I thought it worked for them. They seemed to always have so much fun with each other regardless of all of that. Now that I thought about it, I hadn't really seen the two of them together in the past six months. I just hadn't noticed because I had been so busy thinking about my own marriage.

I finally found some words. "What do you mean it's different? Y'all fuss a lot but you have fun right?"

She sat up. "But that's what I mean. It's like he doesn't listen to me anymore. I know I'm a hell raiser, but he has always said that's what he loved about me. Now, he just ignores everything I say and does whatever he wants without talking to me. It started with that damn humongous ass flat screen that he bought. Remember I told you we had a new one, well he just ran out and bought it without telling me. I came home from shopping, and it was up on the wall."

"Well Cheryl, maybe that's just the man trying to assert some manhood after letting you have your way for so long. I mean, he's wrong for that, but maybe it's not that serious."

A long weary sigh left her lips.

My phone buzzed on top of my desk. I picked it up to see that I had a text from a number that I didn't recognize.

404-333-5555: Looking forward to seeing u in class tonight.

I stared at the phone blankly for a minute.

Cheryl cleared her throat and looked at me pointedly. "Umm, is everything alright?"

I looked up. That had probably been rude of me.

"Oh yeah girl, everything is cool. I just got a text from a strange number..."

It finally hit me who it was. When I signed up for that art class, I'm pretty sure the instructor got a class roster with all of our phone numbers on it. This message was probably from my fine ass art teacher. He was a troublemaker. I was not going to respond.

Cheryl continued talking. "So what you are saying is that it's my fault that we are having these issues because I'm bossy?"

"Now don't put words in my mouth. I didn't say bossy. I'm just saying he has always let you get your way the whole time you have been married."

She looked down at her hands and back at me. "Maybe this is all my fault. I've been so busy. We don't have fun like we used to. You know I work all the time and then I have my consulting business. But it's not all on me is it? He hasn't really said anything to me or confronted me with anything."

I shrugged. "Maybe he has been saying something, and you haven't been listening."

Gallery of Lies

It's so easy to take our spouses complaints for granted. Is that why Mike ignored mine?

Cheryl continued to talk about Ray while we finished up our lunches. I decided that I would not tell her that the guy from the Wing Cafe was my art class teacher. She had her own problems to worry about at home right now. I glanced at my phone again. I deleted the message but saved the contact so that I would know who it was if he contacted me again. At least that's what I told myself. No, I wouldn't respond to that message and as a matter of fact I needed to tell Mr. Art teacher that he didn't need to be texting me. He didn't know if my husband would see it or not, that was just disrespectful. I would just go ahead and clear all of this up when I got to art class tonight.

CHAPTER 6

I WAS RUNNING a little late for class that night. When I walked in, everyone was already there with their supplies out and ready to work. Mr. Art Teacher was already up on the stage getting set up as well. He had his back to the audience. I had hoped to get here a little early so that I could talk to him about the text messages.

JD turned around and faced the class holding his clipboard. He greeted us and smiled.

"I'm glad all of you could make it tonight. This is going to be a good class. First, I'm going to review quickly what we learned on Tuesday. I hope you had a chance to go home and practice a little bit on those techniques. We are going to build on what you learned."

I don't know if I was just self-conscious, but it seemed like he kept looking at me as he talked. I busied myself getting everything ready, trying not to make eye contact. By the time he sat down in front of his easel, I had all of my supplies out and my easel set up to start working. He demonstrated the use of larger brushes on areas of the painting in swirling patterns to create the look of wind blowing. He showed us a stippling technique as well. Then he turned it over to us to work as he walked around the room and coached everyone individually.

I noticed him. I sensed where he was, as if I could feel his presence in the room at all times. He went around to everyone else and spent a few minutes answering their questions and guiding their brushes and showing them things on their own paintings. I should have been working on my own masterpiece instead I was watching him. I quickly turned my eyes back to my paint when

I saw that he was walking towards me. I was the last one that he had come to help. He walked up next to me. My stupid heartbeat sped up. What in hell? I took a deep breath. I didn't meet his eyes.

"So Miss Jacobs, show what you are working on."

He was standing so close to me. He smelled like clean fresh sheets straight from the dryer. Wait... Why in hell was I thinking about sheets?

"I'm working on a painting of a ballet dancer moving across the stage. I have been painting for years, but I always do still life type paintings, so these techniques are new to me."

Was I babbling? I stopped talking and kept painting. Why did I feel nervous?

"Ok, I see. Well what you have here so far is well done. I can tell you have some talent which is something that I can't teach."

My confidence bloomed at the compliment.

"Now your technique is good, but if you flick your wrist a little you can do even better. Let me show you."

I held the brush up to him, but instead of taking it from my hand; he wrapped his big hand around mine and put the brush to the canvas. I sucked in a breath and turned to look at his face. He wasn't looking at me but at the canvas. The heat from his body was warming my side.

I hastily said thanks as I stepped away and pulled my hand out of his. It wasn't until then that our eyes met. A low laugh escaped his throat. What was he laughing at? My nervousness quickly swung to anger.

"What's funny?"

He spoke so low that I could barely hear him. "Nothing is funny. I'm just happy you came to class. When you didn't respond to my text, I didn't know if you were coming tonight."

"Yeah, about that..."

His voice rose over mine as he stepped away and walked back towards the stage. "Ok class. I see everyone is doing well on that technique. We have time to learn one other thing before we wrap up for tonight."

I couldn't believe his arrogant ass. I felt the anger rising up into my chest towards my throat. I kept painting and trying to follow his techniques, but my mind was going through how I would tell him to stop texting me. He was seriously toying with me, and I wasn't going for this.

When the class was finally over, I packed up all my supplies and lingered around so that I would be the last one out.

I stepped towards the stage as JD packed his own things in his saddlebag.

"Look JD. I don't know what game you are trying to play with me, but please don't text me unless it's to inform me of a class cancellation or some other related business. I will tell you again, I am married. Are you trying to cause some kind of trouble for me or do you just get a kick out of trying to get with married women?"

"Miss Jacobs, I wasn't doing anything but giving you a friendly reminder about class tonight. If you saw something more in that text, then I'm sorry about that. I hope I didn't cause a problem with your husband."

"Well luckily he wasn't there to ... well never mind that. I don't need your reminders ok. Let's just keep this professional all right. It was a coincidence that we met before this class started. Don't make more out of it than that. I want to stay in this class and enjoy it, but if you keep doing things like that I will have to stop coming."

He hopped down from the stage and walked towards me. I stepped back.

"I want you to stay in the class. If you don't want me to text you, I won't."

He stepped closer to me again. His hand snaked up and touched my face. I flinched, but I couldn't move. With his thumb, he swiped across my cheek.

Belatedly, I slapped his hand away. "What are you doing?"

He held up his thumb. "You had a drop of paint on your face."

I swiped at it, turned on my heel, and walked out of the classroom.

When I got in my car, I started the engine but sat there for a few more minutes. I had to get my composure. I felt some type of way that I didn't want to face. As I sat there, I saw JD come out of the building and walk over to a motorcycle that I hadn't noticed was there. He fastened his saddlebags to the back of the seat, swung his leg over, and got on. He put the helmet on his head and zoomed out of the parking lot onto the busy street.

I didn't need to come back to this class because when I examined my feelings, I had no problem identifying them. Undeniable lust is what had my temper rising towards this man. I put my car in drive and headed home.

***

I pulled into the garage at my house. When I turned off the ignition, I sat there. It was dark, but I could see JDs face when I closed my eyes. I could still feel the warmth of his hand on mine and I could still smell his scent. I opened my eyes and pulled my phone out of my purse. There were pictures of my husband on here somewhere. Looking at him would erase these images of JD. I scrolled through. There were selfies that I had taken in the bathroom trying out a new lipstick, there were pictures of Cheryl, and I at the comedy show. There was even a picture of my dad that I had snapped while he was asleep in that raggedy chair. I had to scroll a long time to get to pictures of my husband. I looked at his face, a selfie that he had taken with the Grand Canyon in the background. I saw another one he sent me from Phoenix. He was looking solemn in the picture, but I knew every line in his face like it was my own. I stared at the picture until my vision went blurry. JD's face popped into my mind again. I closed the image and hit the call button. Mike had texted me earlier, but he didn't call because he knew I had my art class. He was up in New York, scheduled to come home next Thursday. I needed to talk to him and spend some time with him. I had a conference coming up on Savannah at the end of the month. It would fall on Mike's off days. Maybe he could come with me and we could have a mini vacation, some time with each other is what we needed.

My phone chimed with an incoming text message. I don't know why Mike would text me after I just called him, but I pressed the screen to see it wasn't Mike. The message was from my art teacher.

JD: I'm just making sure you made it home safe.

Damn, this man was hardheaded. Did we not just talk about this? I was not going to respond. I created a new message to my husband.

Me: Call me when you get this.

When I eventually settled down in bed for the night, I still had no response from Mike. The only lights in the room were the tiny LED light on my alarm keypad and on my phone, letting me know it was charging. I picked up the phone and opened the texts to make sure Mike hadn't texted me back. He hadn't. JD's text sat there unopened, and I clicked on it to delete it but found my fingers typing a reply.

Me: Yeah I made it home thanks for checking.

I hit send, and soon after the phone chimed.

JD: I'm glad. Goodnight.

I was tempted to try to carry on a conversation, but that would be stupid. I hadn't talked to Mike so I was really just craving conversation, but JD wasn't a replacement for my husband. I put the phone down and fell asleep seeing images of both men in my dreams.

CHAPTER 7

THE NEXT DAY, I drove my car down the familiar street and rode past trees and houses that were so etched into my memory I did not have to look side to side to see where I was going. I'd driven down these streets so often that I never remembered how I managed to get to the house. I looked up, and I was in the old driveway that was cracked and uneven because of the oak trees roots pushing up from underneath. I always thought of repairing the driveway, but cutting the old and twisted tree was out of the question.

I didn't knock; the front door was open as it had always been on any day that was warm enough that you didn't need a jacket. The black paint on the screen door was peeling, so much so that if you touched it with your hand you would have peppery specks on your skin. I pulled the handle on the door and walked into the dark foyer. I was hit with the smell of old fish grease and stale cigar smoke as I walked past the never used living room on the right. When I walked into the den, I didn't have to look to know that he would be sitting in that old stained burgundy raggedy ass recliner. The chair wasn't even real leather but pleather. It had cracked and peeled so much that he had a blanket folded up in the seat to sit on because it would scratch your legs and leave orange foam on your butt when you got up. I hated that chair and had begged and pleaded for him to let me buy him another one. There's no need to say that I lost that battle.

His back was to me, and I didn't say anything at first. I immediately looked to the wooden tray table to the left of the chair. There was an old glass jar of some type there and in it were a few ice cubes and the remnants of some drink. I had the urge to pick it up and take a sniff to see what the contents were, but I already knew. Next to the glass was a paper plate that held what looked to be half of a fried whiting sandwich. That explained the smell.

I decided to let my presence be known.

"Dad, are you asleep?"

I heard him grumble and then cough. As I walked farther into the room so that he could see me, he shuffled around then quickly reached a hand under the chair before he thought I could see.

"Mona baby, I didn't expect you today."

"Dad I told you that I was going to come by today. You don't remember?"

"Oh baby, it slipped my mind. I would have cooked you some fish. I can still drop you some in the grease if you hungry."

"No thanks, I just ate not too long ago."

There was no telling how old that grease was or where it came from. I was not eating anything that had been floating in it.

"As a matter of fact dad, you know you aren't supposed to be eating anything fried."

"Aww baby, it's just a few pieces of fish. I'll be alright. I was going to have salad for dinner tomorrow."

I rolled my eyes. "Yeah right dad."

I sat on the sofa in front of the T.V. I had bought him the flat panel for Christmas. He'd sworn the old T.V. was just fine but had been grinning from ear to ear when the service people from Home Depot had come and installed it on the wall. This was probably the only thing in the house that wasn't older than me. The sound was turned down so low that you couldn't hear anything the actors said. It looked like he was watching old Matlock reruns. He loved all of those lawyer and police shows for the same reason I hated them. Too much drama and tragedy for me.

"Have you been taking your blood pressure medicine dad? You know you're not supposed to take it with anything but water."

He sucked his teeth the same way I did when somebody told me something that I already knew. "I have been taking my medicine. Ever since I got that pillbox with the days of the week on there, I haven't been missing any more pills. And I know how to take medicine and what to drink. Who you think used to give you your medicine girl?"

I knew he took the pills with water; it was what followed the water that worried me. I didn't want to get into that today, so I didn't say anything. He looked pretty good today like maybe he'd been able to get a full night of sleep last night. He was thin, he'd always been a thin man, but lately his jaws had been looking a little sunken in. I had bitched about the fried fish, but I was glad he was at least eating something. His dark chestnut brown hand went up to his mouth and he fell into a fit of coughing. I didn't go to him because I knew that he would only shoo me away, but I'm sure the frown creases in my face were as deep as a cavern.

"Don't look at me like that. I'm ok and I haven't had a cigar since last Saturday night. I been trying to let them go completely but a man has to have some pleasure don't he?"

He was getting agitated with me. We never talked much. It made me so sad. When I was a little girl, I talked his ear off every day when I came home from school. He used to talk so much more then, telling me about the sights he was on the road in all the towns he visited. But, that was a long time ago when we both slept and smiled a lot more.

"What has your husband been up to? Is he still working on that old car?"

He knew this would set me off and get me to talking. Get the focus off him.

"Well he isn't working on anything. It's just sitting in the garage taking up space that could be used for something else. I keep telling him to sell that heap of junk. All he says is it's a classic, and it would be for someone willing to put in the time and effort to restore it. You know he isn't that handy anyway."

My dad laughed his hoarse laugh. That sound was better than anything that played on the radio, and I didn't hear it enough. He was in good spirits, maybe that wasn't what I thought it was in the glass.

"Well that boy never was that good with tools, always kinda clumsy."

My dad's head was shiny today, which meant he had been to the barber recently. For as long as I have been on this earth, he has been bald. I've seen pictures of him in his teens when he had hair. I always used to tell him that he looked like he was wearing a wig, and he would always inform me that men don't wear wigs. We both got a huge laugh out of my showing him my social studies book in the third grade and pointing out the powdered wigs the men wore as they signed the Declaration of Independence. Clarence with hair just looked so unnatural. He used to shave it himself, but his hand wasn't so steady anymore. Plus, I know that he liked the barbershop for the talk more than anything else. I think that was the only social time he had now.

"Well dad, I just wanted to stop by for a little while and check up on you."

I gathered my purse and stood up. He stood up too. I was taller than my dad by half a foot and today I had on three-inch heels. He hugged me, and I felt him pat my shoulder as was his custom. He looked up into my eyes for a brief second and then looked away. I know it was hard for him to look at me without seeing her sometimes. I had my mother's storm cloud gray eyes that looked even more shocking on me since I had inherited my father's dark complexion. I also had my mother's impossibly thick hair, but where hers had been long and wavy down her back, mine was long and kinky curly more like the ancestors that shared my complexion. When I was in the box at my nine to five, I wore it straight or pulled back in a bun. Today since it was the weekend I'd let it do what it wanted.

"Alright my Monie. I'm going to come to your house soon and look at that water heater."

"Dad I told you I can get someone to do that... "

"Now girl, why would you pay somebody to do that when I've been fixing those things all my life? I told you I'm going to come look at it."

I smiled at him and conceded. I know he needed to do things for me. He had taken care of me my whole life. I know that he would always try to as long as he had breath in his body. He didn't tell me he loved me, but telling me that he would fix the water heater meant the same thing. On the way back down that cracked driveway, I stopped at the old oak tree and ran my fingers over the deeply carved initials, 'C&D', enclosed in a crooked etched valentine. I got in my car, drove away from the past, and tamped down the memories that always threatened to surface. Not today... I didn't want to think about sad things today.

CHAPTER 8

AFTER I LEFT MY dad, I'd called the pharmacy on the ride home and made sure that they had his refills in the system so that I could pick them up sometime later this week. If I didn't pick them up for him, he would use that as an excuse not to take his medicine. When I pulled up in front of my own house and hit the garage door opener, I saw that Mike's truck was already in the garage. I hadn't expected him to be here until around nine tonight. I hope this doesn't mean that he's going to expect me to cook.

I entered the house from the garage and noticed takeout bags on the counter as soon as I hit the kitchen. I didn't feel like eating Chinese, but this was not a battle worth picking. We'd had enough of those already.

"Hey, baby!" He'd walked up behind me and scared the shit out of me. I dropped my purse, and my wallet fell out and popped open, and pennies rolled everywhere. I smacked his arm, and he laughed. He got down on his knees and started to collect the change while I stood there and watched him. I didn't like the look of him crawling around on the floor scurrying like some crab across the floor. I didn't offer to help him pick them up.

Once he held them all, he opened the change clip portion of my wallet, deposited the coins there, and handed my wallet back to me. His face held a tentative smile. I could tell that he wanted to see what mood I was in today. I gave him a small smile back. I looked into the face of the man that I had fallen head over heels in love with ten years ago and saw a glimpse of the young man that he was then. He closed me into a tight hug that told me that he had missed me. After all these years, he still hadn't figured out how not to miss a person so much or at least pretend not to like I did.

"You got here early. What happened? I didn't expect you until about nine tonight."

He stood back and leaned against the counter. "The last client canceled, so I was able to start driving straight home today instead of having to make that stop. I knew you wouldn't be expecting me this early, so I stopped and got some beef and broccoli for dinner."

I was annoyed that he hadn't called and asked me what I wanted instead of just choosing something for me. He proceeded to get the yellow earthenware plates out of the cabinet and take them to the small glass high top table that sat in the breakfast nook. I always sat there most of the time when I was eating alone. It almost felt as if he were infringing on my space. I took my jacket off and hung it on the back of one of the chairs. He put the food on the plates, took two bottles of water from the fridge, and sat down across from me.

He looked at me expectantly. I ignored the look.

"So how was your trip this time?" I asked.

I knew that this would spark a day-by-day account of what he'd done and seen in the three weeks that he was gone. If I let him talk, hopefully he wouldn't ask me how my art class was going. He told me about a few of the clients that he'd seen. He told me of some of the sights that he had seen in Arizona. He'd been to the Grand Canyon. That just pissed me off; he knew that I had always wanted to see the Grand Canyon. He'd been to Hoover Dam and gone to a casino in Vegas. It didn't sound like he had done that much work.

I looked into his tan face as he talked. My husband had always been a handsome man. When I'd met him ten years ago, I had been a senior at UNC Charlotte. I was only a few weeks from graduation and getting my degree, so I had accepted an entry-level job at Wachovia bank in Atlanta, Georgia. I was an intern at the Wachovia banking center in downtown Charlotte when Michael Steven Jacobs had walked through the doors one day in his all brown uniform to deliver a package. It had been a hot day, and he had on the knee length shorts that were common for the drivers to wear in the heat. The first things that I'd noticed were his legs. Lean and muscular, not tiny and birdlike,

I always had admired a man with muscular calves. He wasn't the regular guy that usually stopped in our bank and wasn't quite sure of the routine. He walked up to me at my desk in the lobby and asked if I could sign for a package.

I'd smiled, "Of course I will. Where's Tony, the guy that usually does drops here?"

He handed me the electronic pad and pen so that I could sign. In a clipped voice, he answered as he pulled the pad from my hand and handed me the small package. "Tony got hurt on the job, and I'm taking his route for now."

With that, he turned around and walked out of the door. I was stunned. The brush-off he dealt was abrupt and effective. He hadn't had a smile or anything for me, and I instantly decided that I didn't like him at all. Over the next few weeks, he came into the office regularly. He always stopped at my desk to get me to sign, but after that first meeting, I never had another smile nor had I tried to make any more conversation with him. He'd say hello, ask me how I was doing, or try to make small talk about the weather, but I always kept it to a one-word answer.

Then one day he came in with a package. I'd signed for it, and he'd walked out of the door like every other time before I noticed that it had a fluorescent pink post-it note stuck to the bottom. I still had that post-it note in a scrapbook. It read, "You teased me with that smile the first day I met you, and now you are punishing me because you won't let me see it again. Whatever I did to make you take it away, I'm sorry. Mike from UPS." I think he may have won me over instantly that day. The next time he came in, I had a smile for him. He asked me for my number. We talked and got to know each other and went on a few dates. I came to discover that he was the kindest and sweetest guy that I had ever met. I usually ended up with the bad boys, the arrogant assholes, or the unemployed bums. I knew that Mike would be different.

On our first date, he came to pick me up, and I had worn three-inch heels that made me taller than his six-foot frame. I used to feel ashamed of the height that I had gotten from my statuesque mother. However, I began to relish in the power that I felt. I had learned to embrace it, and many men had told me that with my height and the color of my eyes I was unforgettable. He told me that he loved tall women, and the awe that I saw on his face made me feel like I was in control.

When I graduated and started to make plans to move to Atlanta, he talked of moving too. We had only known each other a few weeks, and I thought that it had to be all talk. What man wanted to be serious so fast? He promised me that things would work out. I moved to Atlanta, started my new job, and we saw each other every other weekend. That was one of the first trials of our relationship. I hated that I only saw him twice a month. I was living in the city where I had grown up, but those times that I was away from Mike had felt completely desolate. I had considered breaking things off with him several times because of that. I had experience with how detrimental loneliness could be, but he told me just to hold on, and things would get better.

I had been back in Atlanta six months before I let him make love to me for the first time. We had gone on an outing to the King museum and talked about the trials of Dr. King and the Civil Rights Movement. We both talked about how the struggle was still so real. I had already experienced too much prejudice in my short time working in corporate America. My white counterparts stereotyped me as the ghetto bitch with a bad attitude because my skin was dark. It hadn't taken long for either of us to become disillusioned with our made for T.V. view of corporate America. As the only person of color in the office, I bristled at the looks I got from white customers when they found out I would be handling their portfolio after they'd assumed I was the receptionist.

Mike managed to find a way to steer the conversation away from work troubles. We'd stopped at Nancy's Pizza after we left there and drove to Piedmont Park to eat it while sitting on the tailgate of his little red truck taking in the lights of the city. He'd kissed me and licked tomato sauce from my fingers.

I'd known then that I was going to let him have my body. We went back to my third-floor apartment furnished with second-hand furniture and do it yourself bookcases that had followed me from my college housing. He laid me down on my king sized mattresses that sat on a frame without a headboard. I let him remove my dress and run his fingers through my hair, and he had looked into my eyes and told me that he wanted me to have his babies someday. I knew that I was in love, and it made me promise that I would do anything for him. He kissed every inch of my body and handled me as if I was made of flower petals. I wasn't a virgin; but when he entered me slowly that first time, it was truly the first time that I had felt love from any man besides my father. I believed he would keep his promises and take care of me. I trusted him completely with everything wild, dark, and damaged inside of me waiting to escape. I knew that he would capture it and calm it before it ran wild. As I lay there and he looked down on me after my orgasm, I counted the light freckles that were scattered on his cheeks and knew that he represented everything that I had dreamed of finding in a man.

After I'd given myself to him, I questioned how the situation would work out. He said that he was working on some things and I just needed to be patient. And I was patient. I waited for him and dated him long distance for damn near a whole year before one weekend that I was visiting him in Charlotte, he told me that his transfer had gone through, and he had gotten a position with UPS in Doraville only a few miles from downtown Atlanta. I was ecstatic. He'd kept his promise and had done what it took to make sure we could be together. He moved to an apartment that was less than five miles from mine, and we continued to date for another year and a half before he proposed to me. My father gave me away in a small ceremony in front of fewer than fifty people at Ebenezer Baptist church. He'd cried as if his heart was broken when the preacher had asked, 'Who shall give this woman away to marry this man?' I had only seen my dad cry one other time, but on that day he was so choked up that all he could do was raise a finger. It had been just the two of us for so long.

Mike and Mona. M&M, our friends called us. Our life had started together and been happy. We had decided to make our home in Mike's apartment while we saved for a house. I had begun to believe that the demons had stopped chasing me. A full night of sleep had eluded me for years, but with Mike by my side, I slept the sleep of contentment. For two years I didn't have one nightmare. We talked about having babies and moving to a bigger place. Mike came home every night and rubbed my feet, and he gave me baths and showered me with love that I soaked up like dry earth in a summer rain.

Then one day, he had come home and told me that he had gotten a great opportunity to make more money that would help us get into our dream home a little quicker. His manager offered him another job in the auditing department that would require some travel. He said it wouldn't be so bad; they had promised that it would only be 25% travel, and it would only be for a year until he found something else. He had promised me, and Mike had always kept his promises.

So, he started his new position, and 25% travel quickly turned into 50% travel and then that turned into me only seeing him about ten days a month. That's when the nightmares had started to come back, on those nights when I attempted to sleep in the house alone. Sleep no longer visited me. I had enrolled in the Master's program at Georgia State University. No one knew that I did most of my studying and research at night while others snuggled in their sheets. It was the only way that I could get away from seeing the terror and anguish on my parents' faces in my dreams.

Mike kept promising me that he would get another position but I knew that he liked the travel. He loved seeing the places that he made his way through. We had bought the so-called dream house that I could not find rest in, but he continued to travel. More than that, I think he liked being away from the ghost that I was becoming. When he did come home, I could never get my sleep to return to me. I walked around the house at night like a poltergeist watching black and white movies and chatting with people on the other side of the world on the internet. He asked me about starting the family we had always talked about, but he was never home. I didn't want to have a child that only knew his father as the man that stopped through town now and then. He promised me that if I got pregnant that he would make things work out.

It had been six years since he had started traveling. I missed my husband, the one that he used to be. I missed the parts of him that I rarely saw anymore. I stopped picking fights and nagging Mike about getting a new job that would keep him home months ago. Maybe in the absence of my angry words, he believed that I finally accepted it.

I let him lead me to the bedroom. He turned back the covers of our marriage bed and laid me down beside him. The hours of foreplay and sex talk had long ago gone out of the door. He kissed me on my neck because he knew that spot turned me on the most. Could I blame him? There was nothing new left to explore. I only felt a particle of the tingle that I had felt for that young boy in the brown shorts. I still loved him, that's what I told myself as I lay there and performed my wifely duties. He entered me without much fanfare. The light from the full moon shone through the big picture window. I looked up at him and could see the concentration on his face.

I closed my eyes and imagined that things were as they used to be. I imagined that on Monday morning he would wake up next to me. Then we would both get into our cars and go to our jobs but on Monday night he would come back home, and I wouldn't have to go to bed alone. My thoughts wandered back to the present, and those old fantasies were enough to make me begin to feel the tremors starting low in my belly. I squeezed my muscles and pulled him deeper into me. The friction was feeling good, and I felt myself getting closer to that cliff, wanting to fall over. I came with a small gasp. Mike pulled me closer and pumped his hips a little faster. His lips hovered above my left ear, and he whispered, "This might be it this time." Then he stiffened and groaned, his seed flowing into me on a wave of his hope.

As I lay up in bed looking down at his serene face as he slept, I looked at those freckles that I used to love to count. Now they just mocked me as they represented each year, each disappointment and each mile of distance, that had come between us. As we had eaten the stupid beef and broccoli that he had brought home, he had finally asked me if there were any signs that I was pregnant. I had not wanted to talk about it because I knew that it would just throw us in a bad place. I told him no and watched the hurt and disappointment that came across his face. It felt like I was looking in a mirror.

I hadn't wanted to sound cold, but I no longer let my emotions run free. I got up from the bed as I did every night about this time and went into the bathroom. I closed the door behind me, reached underneath the cabinet, and pulled the pink plastic pill dispenser from a half-empty tampon box that I kept there. It was Friday, so I lined up the foil package to the right day and pushed the small white pill through the foil. I placed it on my tongue and swallowed. I picked up the tumbler from the counter and filled it with a little bit of water. As I looked at myself in the mirror, I turned the cup up in a toast and washed the pill down with one gulp. Here's to broken promises.

CHAPTER 9

THAT NEXT MORNING and every morning for the next week, the chime of my text message notification awakened me.

JD: Good Morning

The text went without my reply for days. I'd made a mistake when I responded to JD before, and I knew I didn't need to encourage him. In addition to that, Mike came home. That wasn't the sole reason that I didn't reply, but it saved me.

Cheryl and I decided to go on a double date while Mike was home since we hadn't gone on one in such a long time. I suspected that we both had different reasons for wanting this date though I didn't tell her it was because I needed to get another man out of my mind. We decided we would go to this Caribbean style restaurant. The dress I chose to wear was a form-fitting crocheted spaghetti strap slip of a thing in red, green, and yellow. I thought it was appropriate for the island food. I reached way back in the closet and pulled out some of the designer lingerie that I never wore anymore. My ass looked round and sexy encased in the black lace as I twirled in front of the mirror. Mike was taking forever to get ready. He had been unusually quiet since he got home last night. I knocked on the bathroom door.

"Mike, come on, what are you doing in there?" I could hear the buzz of the clippers through the door. Was he cutting his hair?

I decided to go downstairs and have a glass of wine. Fifteen minutes later, he came down wearing tan linen pants and a crisp white shirt. My husband could still turn my head.

"Oh, you look nice."

"Oh thanks," he said. He picked up his phone from the table and looked at the screen with a line in the middle of his forehead.

"So do you like my dress?"

Only then did he look at me.

"Oh yeah babe, you always look gorgeous."

I smiled, and he looked back down at his phone. What the hell?

"Is something wrong?"

He looked up at me again and then put his phone in his pocket.

"Oh nah, babe. It's some stuff for work that I forgot to do. Are you ready to head out?"

Yes, and I was determined not to let his work problems dampen my excitement to go on this date.

Mike helped me climb up into his truck, and we rode to the restaurant. I said some things, tried to ask him about this last trip. His words were spare, so I stopped working to make conversation and looked straight ahead at the little red Honda in front of us. Something was up. I glanced in my periphery and saw his hand go up and press against his temple. It wasn't often that I saw my husband stressed. I didn't want to push the issue. He was probably stressed because he had to take an extended trip and knew I would bitch about it. Tonight though, he was wrong. I was going to try my best not to complain anymore.

If I could train myself to be more like honey instead of vinegar, maybe I could draw this fly to stay home a little more. I wanted to ask Mike about transferring to a different job again, but it was time for a new strategy. It was time to stop letting time pass without dealing with this and trying to make things better. I wasn't happy with my marriage the way it was, but I just read a book that told me happiness is a choice. Could it be that I had been choosing to be miserable? It had been my choice to deny Mike what he wanted, a child.

I had stopped taking my birth control pills. We've been married for ten years now. If we were going to start a family, I might as well give up fighting it. Mike talked to me about having kids, but I had been waiting for everything to be perfect-- For him to do what I wanted. Maybe a baby would be the thing to keep him home and make us both happy.

Cheryl and Ray were already seated with glasses in front of them when we got to the restaurant. They stood as we approached the table, and we swapped hugs. I pointed to the drinks

"Damn, y'all couldn't wait on us?

Ray laughed, "Y'all were taking too long. It's been a hard week; I needed this."

Cheryl smacked her lips. "What's been so hard about this week?"

He stopped laughing, "Dealing with you."

I shot a look at Cheryl. She met my eyes; her lips curled into a smirk. Oh lawd, what was going on with these two? It's like the universe was determined to put me in a bad mood.

We sat down, and I immediately ordered a round of shots. We all just needed to loosen up. I sat so close to Mike that I was almost in his lap. He put his arm around me while he and Ray caught up on life's happenings. We hadn't hung out as couples in so long. I missed this. I thought about what Cheryl had told me about Ray's behavior and found myself watching his actions. He laughed, he drank, he ate, and he talked to Mike and me. His demeanor didn't look too bad to me. Ray put his arm around Cheryl, but she didn't speak much. She smiled and joked a little bit, but it didn't reach her eyes. I would have to get her to come to the ladies' room with me and see what was up after we ate.

When the food came, we all drooled over the jerk wings and brown stew chicken. I had ordered the curry goat. Someone had told me that goat was an aphrodisiac. I fed Mike some from my plate. He chewed, said it tasted good and kissed me on my cheek. It was going to turn out to be a good night. This date is what we needed. Then he looked at his phone and quickly put it back down. I couldn't see what had been on the screen he looked at it so fast. The phone buzzed again on the table, so he picked it up and put it in his pocket. After this, he ate quickly as if this was the last meal he would ever have. His shoulders had tensed up again as they had been in the car. It was Cheryl's turn to shoot me a look. I gave my shoulders a small shrug. What in hell was going on? I had never seen him react this way to a work call.

I downed my drink and ordered another Long Island. Ray finally said something about basketball, and that got Mike talking again. After a few minutes, he excused himself and went to the men's room. I had the feeling he was going to check those phone messages or texts or whatever they were. He was hiding something. When he came back, I grabbed Cheryl, and we went to the ladies' room. I checked under the stalls to see if anyone was in there. Once I saw it was empty, I turned to Cheryl in front of the sink.

"Girl, what's going on with you and Ray? Why are you so quiet?"

She fake laughed. "Oh, nothing. We argued the way over here. I finally rode in that damn car he bought. When he asked me how the ride felt, you know me; I couldn't just say it was smooth. I had to complain again about how he didn't tell me about it. I couldn't let it go. I'm still pissed."

"You probably need a little bit more time. Have you been talking more?"

"No, we haven't had the chance. That's why I was excited about tonight. But it started off wrong from the time we walked out the door."

She dropped her eyes to the floor.

"I started things off on the wrong."

She looked like she had water welling up in her eyes.

"I'm no better. Things aren't going as I planned either. Mike has been dealing with some work issue that has him distracted."

I looked at her in the mirror as I applied more lip-gloss. Cheryl had a funny look on her face.

"Work issue. What kind of work issue?" she said.

"Yeah, he says they keep calling him about something at work. That's why he looks so tense."

"Oh, so he keeps checking his phone for something related to work?"

I paused fluffing my curls. "Well yeah. Mike says his manager keeps contacting him. He's so tense and uptight. UPS is trying to ruin my night. We need to get our freak on tonight girl."

Cheryl then took out her lip-gloss and applied it to her lips, darkening the berry color.

"Let me say amen to that. Ray and I need to get our freak on too. I need to make sure I stay silent all the way back to the house and pretend I'm riding in a Bentley that someone else bought."

We got through the rest of the dinner, but it hadn't gotten any better. I wasn't tipsy, and Mike had killed my vibe. I tried to be quiet on the ride home. I swear I did, but it didn't work.

"Mike, what is going on with you and that phone? What's so important at work that you can't even enjoy a night out with me after being away?"

I don't know if he realized that I could see his face in the shadows in the car. As we passed the streetlights, I could see the muscle in the side of his jaw tighten like he was clenching his teeth.

"I told you, Mona, it's just some stuff with work."

I hated this. He was being evasive.

"What's going on at work? Why don't you tell me about it?"

He cut his eyes at me. "There's nothing to talk about Mona. But--I won't be home for two weeks this time. I have to go and do an audit next week out in Arizona. One of the other auditors quit, and I'm going to have to pick up the slack."

The anger was rising, but I refused to let it come out.

"Oh, so is that what this is about? How long have you known about this two-week trip?"

"I found out a few days ago."

"Is that why you've been acting so shitty?"

He didn't say anything.

"Mike, don't do that. You're not going to ignore me. Answer me. I'm trying to figure out how you have the audacity to act like this towards me when you're the one leaving to take an unscheduled trip. Strange phone calls and texts paired with these excuses. What the hell is happening, are you cheating on me or something?"

The moment I said it I felt guilty. If Mike asked me the same thing, I would say no, I hadn't cheated, but I fantasized about someone else.

"Mona, where is this coming from? You know damn well I'm not cheating on you."

He pulled over to the side of the road and took a long breath before turning towards me.

"Mona, it's nothing like that. Work has me preoccupied, and you are right. I do feel bad for taking another trip. I know you planned for me to be home. I had too. I'm mad about having to work more hours. My manager partnered me with Campbell for this audit. He is almost completely incompetent, so I have to do the bulk of the prep work myself. Baby, I'm sorry that I wasn't much fun tonight."

He took my hand in his.

"I'm tired, Mona. My brain is exhausted."

He turned away from me then but still held my hand while he drove home.

The rest of the car ride was quiet. I rushed to the bathroom to freshen up. Donning my black thong and bra, I slipped into my robe and got the lighter from under the sink to light candles around the room. When I walked out of the bathroom, Mike was in bed wearing his t-shirt. The t-shirt meant 'I'm tired and ready to go to sleep.' I called his name softly, but he didn't stir. His phone rested on the nightstand on his side of the bed, and I was tempted to pick it up and look at it. I didn't. I wouldn't be that woman with my husband. If I wanted to know something, I would ask. Right now, I wanted to know why he didn't want to have sex with me tonight. I started to try to wake him but didn't feel like trying to force him to get in the mood. Not bothering to take my robe off, I got in the bed and turned my back to him. I plugged my phone on the charger and noticed I had a text message.

JD: Goodnight. I hope you sleep well.

I put the phone down and slid my fingers down into my panties. Had I known this how the night would end, I wouldn't have eaten that goat. I brought myself to orgasm, thinking about the man on the other side of that text message while my husband snored next to me.

CHAPTER 10

THE NEXT TUESDAY night in class, meeting JD's eyes had me feeling embarrassed as if he had been a physical part of my fantasizing. Disquiet dampened my spirit that night, and I just couldn't enjoy painting. He walked over to my station and looked at my canvas. His hand rested lightly on the small of my back. Most women knew this to be an intimate gesture, but it also showed possession.

At the end of the class, the mother-daughter dynamic duo that I met the first night in class came over to me.

Val spoke up first. "Hey there Mona, how are you doing tonight?"

"Hey, Val and Tasha. I'm ok."

Tasha spoke, "Girl I was noticing your painting. You have some skills. I mean, you are making the rest of us look bad. Why are you even taking this class?"

"Aww, thanks. I'm really not that good, but I love the art. I just wanted to focus more on my hobbies and have something to do to fill the time."

Tasha laughed. "You don't have to be humble. You're genuinely a good artist. I would hang this on my wall."

Val brushed a gray lock back over her shoulder. She looked pretty with a gardenia pinned up in her hair and a bold red African print skirt that almost touched the floor.

"You need to come and have dinner at my house on Saturday. I plan to have some people over for Tasha's birthday. Come celebrate with us since you looking for things to do to occupy your time."

I probably shouldn't have said that, but now I couldn't be rude. "Oh ok, that sounds like it'll be fun."

Tasha looped her arm through her mom's. "Yeah, I told mama that we could go out this year, but she insists on cooking all of my favorites. I was trying to give her a break."

"No, we aren't going out; I have been cooking your birthday dinner every year since you had teeth to eat it. It's a tradition. Now you can go out to dinner with your other friends another night, but Saturday I'm cooking."

She then turned her face to me. "And you are invited girlie. Give me your phone number so that I can text you the address."

She pulled a phone out of her pocket and handed it to her daughter.

"Put her number in there for me."

I called out my number, and my phone immediately rang over by my easel.

"I just called you from this number so you can save it." Then Tasha pulled out her phone and tapped the screen, and my phone chimed again. "And now I have you saved, and you have my number also. I'll give you a call. You should come and hang out with us sometime."

We headed back to our stations and packed up our things. The ladies waved at me as they left the room. I shoved my tools in my bag and walked on out to the bathroom. I didn't want to linger around class too long tonight. I needed to talk to Mike and clear some things up with him. When I got out to the car, my phone rang, and Mike's picture popped up on the screen.

"Hey," I said.

"Hey baby."

"Mike, I couldn't stop thinking about the other night when we went out to dinner. You know I don't like to talk about the fact that you travel so much anymore because I don't want to argue with you. But, it feels like we are getting even more distant. We didn't even have sex that night. That's not like you after being away from me."

Mike didn't say anything for a long time, so long that I thought the call had dropped.

"Hello... Mike?"

"I'm here... I felt bad about that night the whole time I have been out here in Arizona. There's so much going on and it's got me stressed the fuck out. I'm overwhelmed."

I grew concerned. "What's going on? You haven't let this job stress you out like this before. Now might be a good time to switch things up if UPS has you feeling this way. There are so many companies that you could work for."

"I know Mona. You're right. It's time for me to change some things, I just don't know how. I don't know what I need to do next... It's not just the job, there are other things too. I'm so scared to disappoint you even more Mona. I need to tell you..."

I cut him off. "Disappoint me even more? What's that supposed to mean? If you changed jobs in order to be here with me more, how could that possibly disappoint me? I'd be so happy. Mike please consider it this time. I can help you find something. I want us to be close again. I miss us so much."

There was another long pause.

"Mike?"

When he spoke again it was just above a whisper.

"Yes, Mona, I'm here. I miss us too. I'm going to fix everything soon, I promise. I love you so much Mona, I want you to always remember that.

CHAPTER 11

SATURDAY AFTERNOON emerged with warm breezes that tickled the skin and sunshine that prompted me to reach for the dark black sunglasses that I kept on my visor. The sunroof and windows of my car all stood open. I was sure the drivers next to me at the red light could hear the 80's R&B music spilling from my speakers. When I pulled into dad's driveway and blew the horn, he stepped out so quickly that he had to have been waiting by the door for me to arrive. He dapped down the steps and got into the passenger seat before leaning over to kiss me on the cheek.

"Hey, Monie."

"Hey, Daddy. You look nice."

He was wearing a dark blue Kangol cap and another one of his Stacy Adams shirts, this one in blue with a pair of jeans.

"Thanks, baby, these are the jeans you bought me for my birthday a few years ago."

I turned a corner grinning to myself.

"And I bet this is the first time you've ever pulled them out of the closet, right?"

His raspy laugh made me feel light and happy.

"Well, you know me. I need to have someplace special to wear my good clothes. Now, tell me, where exactly are we going again? You know I was planning to go up to the barbershop today."

"Didn't you just go and get a haircut Wednesday?"

"Yes, but I wasn't going for a haircut, I need to go back up there and win my money back that I lost on the spades game. I didn't know Otis was a terrible spades player. He will never be my partner again."

I just shook my head. There's no telling what they did and talked about up at that barbershop. I made sure to stay out of there. I didn't need those dirty old men staring at my booty.

"Well dad, we are going to a get- together at one of my art classmates' house for a birthday. I guarantee you there'll be some folks your age there. Don't worry. I think it will be fun and from what I heard there'll be plenty of food."

I glanced over at him with his lip turned up in the corner-- a look that mirrored my own when I was skeptical about something.

I drove down the unfamiliar street and instantly loved the feel of the neighborhood. There were lots of sturdy brick homes and mature oak trees lining the street. Children's playhouses and toys littered many of the front yards. On one side, kids played in the sprinklers with a big shaggy dog. It reminded me of the neighborhood that my aunt had lived in when I was a little girl, where I'd sometimes go play. My GPS told me that the house was coming up on the left and I parked behind some other cars lining the street. It looked like they had a good crowd in there by the number of vehicles up and down the road.

Soft music ebbed from the dusky blue bungalow. The house looked just as open and friendly as Val's personality. Two square white columns held up a porch that housed a swing and two outdoor chairs. I could imagine having tea out here on a spring day with the breeze blowing the leaves of the pear tree. Tea rose bushes and azalea bushes flanked the two brick stairs that lead up to a bright red front door. There was a doorbell as well as an old-fashioned door knocker. I decided to use both, and it wasn't long before a young girl of about twelve came to the door smiling. She was skinny, nothing but knees and elbows in her blue sundress.

"Hi there," she said. "Come on in." I walked into a foyer with mustard-colored walls. The girl offered both dad and I a small hand for a very mature handshake.

"I'm Tiffany, Val's niece. Everybody had their hands occupied, but she's in the kitchen putting the finishing touches on dinner. Follow me."

I couldn't say anything but ok before Tiffany turned back around with her brown curly hair swaying between her shoulder blades. We entered a living room where people sat everywhere there was room for a seat. Children played a game of tic-tac-toe in the middle of the floor. My eyes searched the room for a familiar face to finally land on Tasha's. She jumped up out of her seat, came over to me, and embraced me in a hug. She looked radiant in a yellow maxi dress that brought out the gold tones in her skin. She wore her dreads twisted in an elaborate style that looked like something out of a natural hair magazine.

"Heeeyyyy Mona. I'm so glad that you could make it. Now, who's this handsome young man?"

"Tasha, this is my dad."

She broke into a big grin and gave him a quick hug as well. Dad's lips curved into a smile back at her.

"You can just call me Clarence and thanks for allowing me to come to your celebration."

He had told her to call him Clarence which was a good sign. When he didn't like the look of someone, he said to call him Mr. Thomas.

She then turned towards the kitchen and yelled: "Hey Mom, Mona's here."

A few seconds later, Val came from behind a door wearing a kente cloth printed apron with her hair was pulled up onto a loose ball on the top of her head.

"Hey there girl, I'm so glad you could make it. And you brought a guest."

Tasha chimed in, "Yeah mom, and this is Mona's dad, Clarence."

Dad tilted his chin down and reached out to grasp the hand that Val offered.

"I already know this is going to be a great party with these beautiful ladies running things."

Val laughed. Actually, I think it was more of a giggle. She reached up and swatted his hand.

"Aww, look at you trying to score points with flattery. It worked. Anyway, dinner is almost ready so let me get back in the kitchen. Tasha, get these folks something to drink. We have some appetizers too. Y'all, help yourself."

With that, she whipped back around the corner. My dad's eyes passed quickly over Val's form as she sashayed back to the kitchen. I looked away before he saw me watching him. I hadn't seen my dad try to flirt with a woman in ages. Tasha pointed to a coffee table loaded down with a fruits and cheeses. On a sideboard stood a big punch dispenser filled with pink liquid.

"Mona and Clarence, help yourselves to the appetizers. I'll fix you a drink. Would you like some regular punch or some of this extra special adult punch?" As she said this, her finely arched eyebrows bounced up and down. I couldn't help but laugh.

"I will take some adult punch."

"Yes, it's sooooo good. I made it real special so you may not want to drink it too fast," she said with a giggle.

Dad spoke up, "I'll take some regular punch."

She went over to the side and got plastic cups from the stack, filled them with ice and poured orange liquid from an enormous pitcher that sat over to the sideboard. After placing the drink in my hand, she poured dad a cup of the pink punch from the dispenser.

"Let me introduce you to everyone." Everyone in the room seemed to be embroiled in a deep conversation, and I had the feeling that they hadn't even noticed that we had come in.

"Hey y'all, this is Mona and her dad Clarence. She's in the art class that mom and I are taking --the one that she doesn't need to be in because she's already some kind of Van Gogh or something. This pretty lady is my Aunt Rosa, and this is Uncle Bo." The woman had to be Val's sister because she was a clone of her, but with a short faded haircut. She wore beautiful big wooden earrings that I instantly wanted for myself. Next were Uncle Jimmy and his daughter Serena. There were several of Tasha's cousins, Steve, Chris, and his girlfriend, Kim. We met two of Tasha's co-workers, Shana and Angel. Then she turned to a slim man wearing glasses.

"And last but not least this is my boyfriend, Brandon."

He smiled and stood up to be at least 6'6". He shook my hand and dapped up dad before lowering his body back down into his chair, leaving an empty one on the other side of Tasha for me to sit down. Dad walked over and took an empty chair next to Uncle Henry. Her aunts and uncles all smiled and welcomed us to the party. Then they started up again with a story of Tasha making a 'mud' pie out of doggy poop when she was a little girl. Tasha's face turned rosy up to the roots of her hair.

Gallery of Lies

"See, y'all are so wrong. Why do you people always tell these embarrassing stories when company comes around?"

Brandon put his arms around her shoulders. "You better be glad I already fell in love with you or that story might have changed my mind."

She slapped his arm and burst out laughing. The family asked the usual questions about us. I gave them the typical snapshot of my life that everyone always wanted to hear about my successful job and my handsome husband. It all sounded so great when I told people about it. A few minutes later Val stepped out of the kitchen and yelled that dinner was ready.

"Can I get some help setting it out?"

Aunt Rosa, Serena, and Kim got up to help. I stood up, and so did Tasha.

"Is there anything I can do to help?"

Val tsked, "No girl. You and Tasha just stay over there out of the way. I can't have the guest and guest of honor in here helping like I don't know how to be a host. But you men can move some of those chairs over here to this table so everybody can sit down."

The men, including my dad, immediately jumped into action as the ladies started coming out of the kitchen with dish after dish of food. Who was going to eat all of this? We took our seats at the table where everything looked so good. The fare represented a mix of Caribbean and traditional southern dishes. Cabbage, oxtails, brown stew chicken, and peas and rice filled rainbow colored platters. She sent out fried chicken, collard greens, and macaroni and cheese along with coco bread and pound cake. I was going to hurt myself trying to eat all of this food because I intended to sample everything.

Uncle Bo sat at the head of the table and asked everyone to join hands while he blessed the food. While everyone started to pass dishes around and dig in, I sat back to take it all in. I looked over at dad sitting next to me, complimenting Val on how good everything smelled and looked. I loved being around big close families like this, but it made me think of how I had missed out on these kinds of gatherings in my own family. Most of the time, it was just my dad, Mike, and me. Sometimes Mike's mom, Suzie, would come down to visit but she didn't like to make that drive from Charlotte much anymore. Even when we went to visit her, it was usually just the three of us unless Mike's sister was also in town.

Since my aunt had died, my dad didn't spend much time with his other family members. She had been the one to host the dinners and cook all of the food for the holidays. We never saw my mother's family anymore. Sometimes I talked to my grandmother, but in a way, I always felt that she didn't want to have much to do with us after my mom died.

When we started to wind down on dinner, Val disappeared into the kitchen and came back out with a white frosted cake with candles on it. She started singing "Happy Birthday" as everyone joined in. Tasha had tears in her eyes as she blew out the candles.

"I just want to say that there isn't much more I can wish since I have all of you guys here with me to celebrate my birthday. It is truly a blessing to have all of you in my life."

After dinner, we played a game of Taboo in teams, boys against girls. I joined in, and everyone cheered me on as I got up to give my set of clues. I hadn't had this kind of fun in a long time. When I guessed one answer, Aunt Rosa slapped me a high five as she did a little hip shimmy when we racked up more points than the men. Dad and Uncle Henry didn't join in Taboo. The two bachelors sat in the corner having an intense debate about politics and something about Muhammed Ali's activism over a checkerboard.

The party started to wind down around seven. I looked for dad and found him in the kitchen saying something to Val that had her head thrown back with laughter as she handed him a plate wrapped in aluminum foil. Everyone gave us hugs as we announced we were leaving. I heard Uncle Henry invite my dad to his monthly poker game while I thanked Val again for the invitation. Dad was all smiles as we got in my car. We waved at Val and Tasha who stood in the front door of the bungalow as I pulled away from the curb. It had been a long time since I had that much fun. Dad chattered on and on about how good of a cook Val was as we drove back to his house. It had been a good day, and that reminded me how much I missed family.

CHAPTER 12

TUESDAY NIGHT arrived and art class was all about technique and contained no surprises. That is until it was time to go home. I turned the key in the ignition. The car made a few whining noises and then stopped. I knew that sound. Dammit, I had somehow drained my battery. I looked up at the overhead light switch and saw that I had left it on. I sat back in my seat and closed my eyes for a minute while I berated myself for being stupid. It was dark, and I had stood beside my car talking to Mike on the phone and let everyone from class leave out of the parking lot. I looked over near the door and saw that JD's bike was still out front. However, he had a bike, so my jumper cables wouldn't do me any good. I took my phone back out of my purse and called roadside assistance. Of course, they could send someone out, but they were at least forty-five minutes away. You would think in the city it wouldn't take so long for someone to arrive.

I leaned back in the seat and closed my eyes. A knock on the window scared the shit out of me. JD stood there motioning for me to let my window down. I opened the driver's side door and yelled since there was no power for the windows.

"My battery is dead!"

He walked around to my side and stood next to the door.

"Oh ok. I was getting ready to leave and saw you sitting out here. I'm just checking to see if everything was ok. Maybe we can try to flag someone down to get them to jump your car."

"No, I'm fine. I already called roadside assistance. The woman on the phone said it would be about forty-five minutes, so I'll just wait."

He ran a hand over his beard.

"You might as well come on back inside the building then. It's not safe for you to sit out here in your car by yourself. I'll just wait with you. I have a Keurig in my office; I'll make you a cup of coffee."

"Believe me; it's cool. I will just wait out here. You can head on home."

"Well if you don't want to come inside, I'll wait out here with you. I'm not leaving a woman to wait out here by herself. Unlock the door. He walked around to the passenger side of the car and put his hand on the handle."

What in hell? There was no way I was going to sit in the close confines of my car with this man. How would that look if someone saw us anyway? It would look like we had parked here to make out. Oh hell no.

"You know what, you're right." I said.

I grabbed my purse off the seat and got out of the car. He had a point; there was no need for me to compromise my safety trying to avoid him. We walked back into the building. Instead of going straight into the classroom, JD turned to a door on the left side of the hallway. I had never really even paid any attention to it. When he opened the door, behind it stood a small office space that held a desk and a bookshelf full of art books and supplies. I could tell that he didn't spend much time in here, but on a table to the side, there was the promised Keurig machine along with a basket of k-cups, creamers, and sugar. From a shelf above the table, he took two down two foam cups and proceeded to make us both a cup of coffee. While he brewed the delicious smelling liquid, I sat in the chair in front of his desk. The room's walls were painted institutional gray while on the standard issue brown 1980's wood-like desk rested a fake plant and a printer. A cork board behind the desk held our class roster and some advertisements for other classes that he had taught or would teach in the future.

"This stuff in this office was already here when you leased this building wasn't it?"

He laughed. "Yeah, you can tell?"

I raised an eyebrow. "Definitely. This room doesn't have any personality, and I can't imagine that you would have purchased this stuff; especially the fake plant."

He handed me a cup of coffee.

"You're right; this office already sported this unique decor. Only the books came with me. I use this office sometimes when I have a class going on, and I need to print something. I actually run my business from an office at home. Come on, let's go into the studio, I want to show you something."

He walked past me and out the door of the tiny room. I got up and followed him back to the studio. He put his stuff down by the door, and I put my purse down. He surprised me by walking over to my painting. I hesitated but finally walked up next to him.

"Are you about to criticize my painting? I don't think I can deal with that right now."

He turned to me and laughed. "No, I just want to show you something. You know, your painting is exceptional. I don't say too much about it in class because I don't want to make the others feel bad, but you are the best artist in this group. You have an eye for the details that others miss."

My cheeks felt warm.

"You see right here where you were filling in the horse's legs... Wait let me get a brush."

He jogged over to the supplies and quickly got a small brush and squeezed some paint on a palette. He handed me the brush.

"I could tell that you were getting frustrated with how the legs look flat and motionless. You have done an excellent job on the body, but it's just a play on how you show the light hitting them. Dapple that lighter yellow kind of near the back of the legs."

I touched the brush to the canvas, unsure of what he was telling me to do. He put his hand on top of mine, and that tingling sensation was back just like when he had touched me before. He helped me to press the brush to the image. When he pulled his hand away, I could see the effect of the change precisely as he had described.

"Oh, this is awesome. I didn't know how to get this effect. I kept trying to make the legs darker; I would never have thought to use the yellow."

I dipped my paintbrush into more paint and tried to imitate the technique that he had just shown me. My fingers maneuvered the brush, and I stippled the paint slowly at first. Then as I saw that the method made the painting come alive, my fingers moved with more confidence.

"You're doing an awesome job, Mona."

I had almost forgotten JD was there, but when his warm breath feathered across my ear, I became in tune with the proximity of his body behind me. He reached around me once again and grasped my hand in his.

"Now take a little of this red and mix it with the yellow and create some shadows where you just put the yellow."

He looked over my right shoulder and moved so close to me that his front brushed against my back. His left hand settled on the other side of me on my waist, his fingertips grazing my stomach. There was no space between us at all. I couldn't find the words to object to his forwardness. My hand followed his guidance without hesitation. I wasn't thinking. I could only feel. The colors on the painting were starting to vibrate and take on a life of their own. I added shades of red that elevated my art to a new level, and the sensations trickling through me made me feel reckless.

"Do you see what a difference just that small thing made in your picture? You do have the eye; I'm impressed by how quickly you learn."

He took the brush from my fingers and put it down on the edge of the easel. Then his fingers tightened around my waist as he turned me towards him. He reached around me to the stool next to my easel, grabbed a cloth from the table, and proceeded to wipe paint from my fingers and his. I let him clean me and he put the rag down. We both stood there, and then he tilted my chin up and put his mouth on mine. The kiss thrilled me. It was as if a door opened that I had been trying to keep locked. I leaned into the kiss. His arms came around me, his big body engulfing me. His warm hand was on the back of my neck, and I didn't want him to stop. Just enjoy the kiss I thought. Mike had ignored me, worried more about whatever was happening with his job or whatever business he had been trying to handle the other night instead of being with me. I wanted this attention. I wanted to feel loved.

The jingle of my phone ringtone snatched me out of the kiss. I looked around feeling disoriented, yanked myself out of JD's arms and rushed over to the table where my purse rested. The phone had fallen to the bottom of my bag. When I answered it, my voice sounded funny to my ears. The technician told me that he was pulling up to the address and asked me which car was mine. JD started towards me, and I snatched my purse up before he could say the thing I could read on his face.

"Roadside assistance is outside. I need to get out there and see where he is."

With that, I turned and walked out of the classroom as fast as I could without running. What had just happened? How could I let him kiss me like that? Outside, the technician drove around in a white pickup truck with a magnetic sign emblazoned with big black letters identifying it as Roadside Rescue. I pointed him towards my car and turned to see JD walking over towards us. I couldn't meet his eyes. That kiss had felt so incredible with his body pressed against mine. The technician hopped out of the truck. He was a short, middle-aged man that introduced himself as Jose. After opening the toolbox on the back of his truck, he returned with a portable battery charger and looked at the both of us, probably assuming we were together.

"Can you pop the hood?" Jose said to neither of us in particular.

I jumped in and pulled the lever to release the hood. Jose lifted the hood and hooked up the cables. JD stared at me, but I was determined to avoid his gaze. Jose charged the battery with the portable device then he closed the hood, gave me a receipt, and drove away. JD stood there waiting until Jose was out of sight.

"Mona, look at me. I know that what happened back there caught you off guard, but I won't say I'm sorry it happened because I'm not."

He reached for my hand, but I pulled away.

"JD, don't do that. You shouldn't have kissed me." I said.

"I know you're feeling me like I'm feeling you. There's been something between us since that first night we met at Karaoke, and you were singing to me."

I ran my hand through my hair. "You're right JD, I'm feeling something, but... wait, what? I was not singing to you."

He laughed and took the opportunity to move closer to me again. I didn't stop him when he took hold of my hand this time. I didn't back away.

"No, I'm convinced you were singing to me. I saw how your eyes locked on me in the back of the room."

He was smiling at me with those perfect white teeth gleaming against his brown lips. What would happen if I gave in to these desires and didn't think about consequences? People do it all the time. He wrapped me in his arms again, and I let myself enjoy it. There was no telling what my husband was doing right now. He probably already had someone out there on the road. He was probably with them at this very moment. I pulled myself out of JD's arms.

"JD, I have to go. No matter what I feel or what you feel, this isn't right."

He stepped back. "If you want me to leave you alone, I will."

I drove home in silence so that I could think. I didn't want JD to leave me alone. I was already beyond tired of my husband leaving me alone. That night when I got home, Mike didn't call me at the usual time, and I didn't call him either. What I did was think about how long it was going to be before I saw JD again and how the next time I wouldn't stop him.

CHAPTER 13

THE DAILY TEXT messages continued. Text messages turned into phone calls. We talked about other things besides what was happening between us. JD became the person that I talked to about my day at work and the battles I continuously fought for recognition. We flirted over the phone, and we laughed and talked about silly things like motorcycles and music and serious topics like politics and finances. We did not, however, discuss our personal lives or the people in them.

In class, the tension between us kept building. I hoped that no one noticed. I felt as though JD spent a little too much time at my easel when he roamed around the class giving one on one instruction. He touched my hand, or he brushed against my body as he passed me.

Thursday night, after class walking to my car, I got a text from him.

> JD: Come with me somewhere.

> Me: Like where?

> JD: Highland Cigar Co

> Me: I don't know if that's a good idea.

I unlocked my door and reached to open it when I heard JD's motorcycle crank and then rumble to life. To my astonishment, he revved up the bike and drove straight for me. He lifted the visor of his helmet.

"Come on and go with me. I won't keep you out too long."

He turned, lifted the seat behind him, and pulled out another helmet.

I laughed, "Oh, you want me to ride with you on that thing. No, I don't think so. I need to get on home and besides; my hair is not going to fit under there."

He tugged at my hand. "It's not that far, only a few blocks down the road... And your hair will fit."

I hesitated with my hand still on my door handle.

He sensed that I wanted to go. I had always wanted to ride on a motorcycle. Before I could change my mind, I took the helmet from his hand and crammed my hair under it until it fit. I put my bag across my body and slung my leg over the seat.

"Just put your arms around my waist and lean into the turns with me."

As soon as I got into position, he leaned forward and revved the motor. The tires sped over the asphalt, and it seemed fast to me, but I had the feeling he was holding back a little not to scare me. When he turned, I squeezed my thighs against him and pressed my breasts against his back. When it was time, I leaned into the turns as he had instructed. The ride ended way too soon as he slowed to a stop and pulled into a parking space already occupied by a gray Harley Davidson. My heart thudded, and I was sure he could feel it against his back. I couldn't stop smiling as I took the helmet off and handed it to him. That short ride was one of the most thrilling things I had felt, ever. He stood up from the bike and looked down at me.

"By that smile on your face, I'm guessing you liked that ride."

I couldn't help but laugh. "Hell yeah, I liked it."

"Well, damn, you might be a speed demon." He laughed and gripped my hand in his. I didn't want to make it awkward by pulling away, so I let him hold it and lead me into the bar.

We sat on the low leather couch touching thighs and shoulders drinking cognac. I had smoked cigars before, but I was an amateur at it. I ordered one that was supposed to taste like coffee, and he went for the bigger, stronger ones that I couldn't pronounce. My hair was going to smell like smoke, but I didn't care. We conversed, and I settled into the crook of his arm as he nuzzled my ear. Those sort of outings became our new ritual. Those evenings after the art classes, we would get a drink somewhere different. Somewhere I thought I wouldn't see anyone I knew. He made me laugh so much with his stories of when he used to be the president of the bike club I had seen him with when we first met. Now, as a founder of the club, he was an honorary lifetime member. These days though, he told me that he mostly rode solo.

The night of the last class came with trepidation. I didn't want it to end. I had found a passion for the art that I didn't know I had, but I had also found a passion for JD that I never thought would develop. When the classes ended, I would no longer have anything to look forward to on those Tuesday and Thursday nights. Our ritual of meeting up after class would be over. At the close of the session, each person expressed thoughts on what they had learned while JD gave all of us certificates of completion. He let everyone know that the next class in the series would start in three weeks for those that wanted to continue. I thought about signing up so that I could still see him. I didn't know what I was going to do. As we left out, Val and her daughter gave me a warm hug. I promised to keep in touch so we could all get together again. When it was all over, I walked to my car on the verge of tears. I waited for the text, and finally, my phone chimed.

JD: No bar tonight. I want to show you my studio.

I hopped on JD's bike and after a short ride, we cruised into a parking deck. I had driven past this building many times on my way to work. This old Cotton Mill from the 30's had been converted to residential lofts. I knew it contained some pricey residences and had always wanted to see the floorplans and decor inside. He parked his bike in a narrow space next to a black Range Rover. He got off the bike and took my hand to lead me through a door into a modern, industrial decorated lobby with exposed pipes snaking through. The walls stood covered with abstract art, and the furniture looked like the kinds of things you would buy from IKEA. We got on the elevator, and the anticipation had me trembling inside. He told me all about his studio in the conversations we had over wine and bourbon.

When he unlocked the door, he urged me to enter in front of him. I walked into a brick-lined space with sky-high ceilings crisscrossed with burnished steel beams. The kitchen lay to the left of the entrance, laced with black granite and stainless steel surfaces. He opened a cabinet and pulled out two glasses and a bottle of bourbon. With my drink in hand, I took in my surroundings. The living space was open, the glazed concrete floor covered with colorful handwoven rugs that seemed like they would have clashed but worked in the area with the leather furniture. It looked like I expected JDs place to look. It emitted masculinity and passion with larger than life paintings covering the walls, leaving no area bare. Abstract works and paintings of the city's streets hung at all heights on the brick. The most magnificent piece depicted a group of five men with helmets in hand, standing next to their crotch rockets against the city background. I recognized JDs blue and silver bike amongst the other ones of black, yellow green and red.

I stood in awe of this man's talent.

"Why isn't this stuff in a gallery?" I asked.

He watched me as I looked at his art. His face held motionless, the way one looks when waiting for judgment. It must have been a struggle to stand there and let someone see the creative workings of your soul laid bare.

"Your work is awesome JD. I knew you could paint. Obviously, you teach a class, but I had no idea how good your work is."

His face relaxed into a smile as he walked up and put his arm around my waist in front of the painting.

"I'm glad you like it, Mona, you don't know how much I wanted to impress you."

I laughed, "Mission accomplished."

He showed me the rest of the space. Upstairs, an area held his easel and paints in front of a bank of floor to ceiling windows. The view of the city was extraordinary. He put his phone on a dock and the loft filled with music. He started to pull out paints and brushes.

"Let's paint something together." He said.

I stood at the easel, spreading the paint on the canvas with my brush just using colors and feelings. This motion was what abstract art was about, feeling. The colors were gold and copper and crimson. I wasn't thinking about what I painted but let my senses guide me. He walked up behind me and put his arm around my waist.

Maxwell played in the background: I want you to prove it to me in the nude Addicted to the way you move

His hand covered mine and held the brush with me. He kissed the back of my neck. My eyes closed but the brush continued to glide on the canvas. He swayed with the music. I moved my hips with his. Oh God, this was getting out of control. He took the brush away from me and turned me to face him.

He was kissed me. Sucking on my bottom lip; his hands went under my shirt, to my breasts. My hands stroked his back and then rested on either side of his face. I saw that I smudged paint on his cheek.

He pushed my shirt up and pulled it over my head. The cool air hit my skin, but it didn't stay cool long as he kissed my neck and my breasts. He laid me down on the rug in front of the easel. He held himself over me, the weight of him feeling glorious to my body.

Maxwell's sensuous voice weaved through the air. I tugged at his shirt, and he helped me to get it over his head. With his arms around me and our bodies pressed together, I couldn't think. He kissed my thighs. His pants came off, and I ran my hands over the muscles in his stomach. He reached up and got the paintbrush. He swirled the paint around my belly button and my nipples teasing me until I panted his name in shallow breaths. I wanted him so badly that all doubt and hesitation was gone. When he entered me, our skin was slick with paint and sweat. He held my hands over my head and kissed me while he stroked me deeper and deeper.

He flipped me over to my stomach, and I could feel him painting the notes of the music down the center of my back. He kissed my shoulders and painted the notes on the back of my thighs before he took me from behind. As he filled me, it wasn't long before I balanced right on the edge, waiting for him to push me over. I teetered on the cliff with him, holding me on the verge of sweet release. I jumped, and it was too late to turn back.

CHAPTER 14

I SORTED THROUGH the clothes in my laundry room as JD's voice murmured in my ear over my Bluetooth.

"What time are you leaving out tomorrow?"

I pressed the start button the washer. "I am going to leave out at about five, right after I leave work. I'm trying to get these clothes washed and packed so that I can leave straight from work without coming home first."

"Well, I don't have to work this weekend, why don't I come with you?"

I hesitated. Did I want him to come with me? I had thought Mike would travel with me when I booked the room months ago, but that wasn't going to happen now was it? I must have taken too long to answer because he spoke up again.

"You don't want me to come? What, are you afraid someone will see us together?"

"Well... It's not that really. I don't know." I said.

"It's cool. Let me get back to work, my team lead is calling me on the radio." He said, sounding a little hurt.

"Ok, bye." I said and he hung up.

I went in my closet and chose a charcoal gray suit for my meeting on Friday. I picked and a pair of navy slacks with a floral top for the Saturday morning meeting and put them in my suit bag. I had only known JD for four weeks. Did I want him going to Savannah with me? It could be a sticky situation if I ran into anyone, but there would only be a few other people from my office at this conference. It could be a lot of fun. Since I had been living dangerously, I decided to keep it going. I never wanted to go to this thing by myself anyway, but Mike had bailed on my plans.

I typed a quick text to JD and hit send.

Me: I want you to come, pack for four days.

JD: I'll be ready baby.

The rental company had dropped off my car at lunchtime. I was headed out the door when I ran into Cheryl in the hallway. I didn't want to talk to her right then.

"Hey girl, so I guess you are headed off to the Marketing and Sales Roundup. Why do you guys always get all the perks while we bean counters are left here to keep things running?"

"Girl, I would gladly let you go in my place. These folks act like I want to spend the weekend with them. Not only are classes on the agenda, I have to go to dinner with these fools. You know they get on my nerves. Other than that, I will probably be sitting in my room catching up on work." I couldn't meet her eyes with that lie.

Cheryl laughed, "You know I'm playing. This is a bad time for me to go anywhere, plus I'm going to see my mom this weekend. But you should try to have some fun on the company's dime while you're there. Do some shopping and remember that your best friend's birthday is coming up and she loves handmade jewelry."

We both laughed before a quick hug. She walked away and I immediately felt bad for lying to my friend, but I couldn't let her know what I was really going to do this weekend.

When I got outside, I put my luggage in the car and drove to JD's loft. In front of the building, I called him and told him I was outside.

He opened the passenger door and folded his big frame into the seat. I'm glad I had requested an SUV or his knees would have been on the dash. He leaned over and turned my face towards him for a kiss. I pulled back. It wasn't like that was it? Besides anyone that I knew could see us in the city, he knew better than that. I leveled a firm look at him.

"Come on now," I said with the side eye.

He laughed, "I forgot baby. I will keep my lips to myself until we get out of town."

I didn't think it was funny.

As I drove to Savannah, the conversation was entertaining though I didn't tell him too much personal information about myself. I talked about a few of the adventures Cheryl and I had when we were in college. As I mentioned her name, I felt like an awful friend for keeping this from her, so I quickly changed the topic. He talked about his day job as an engineering project manager, so maybe he could afford that condo. JD told me a whole lot about him and didn't seem to mind that I didn't get too personal, that is until he asked me the wrong questions.

"So, tell me, do you want to leave your husband?"

I was mute for a minute. "No, I do not want to leave my husband. Why are you asking me about him?"

"I'm just asking because I want to know how I play into this equation. It's clear that dude is gone all the time, and you're lonely. Otherwise, I wouldn't be here."

I may seem irrational, but his words made me angry. How dare he assume to know me?

"Well, we never made a verbal agreement, but we both know what this is right?" I said.

I waved my finger back and forth between us. "This, whatever this is, is just a way to fill my time. You understand that right? If I leave my husband or stay, it will not have anything to do with you."

Internally I cringed. Is this how men talked to their mistresses? I held the power to cut this off if I wanted to though. I hope he knew that. He had not said anything else and looked straight ahead. I hoped that would be the end of the conversation, mainly because I didn't want to face the person I'd become.

The tension lessened as we made the rest of the four-hour trip to Savannah. It was about 9:45 P.M. when I checked into the hotel as JD walked over to the bar area and looked around. He had caught on that he should be discreet. I glanced around the lobby, screening for any familiar faces. There were none. I was glad, that would mean no problems for us. I let the concierge load the bags onto a trolley. As I walked towards the elevators, JD ambled up and joined us as the doors opened. When we got to the room, and the concierge unloaded the bags, I was reaching into my purse for a tip when JD stepped up in front of me and handed the man a bill. I didn't see how much. I appreciated the gesture.

I stepped out of the room to call Mike and let him know that I had made it to Savannah. As he asked me about the drive and I felt a twinge of guilt but quickly tamped it down. I was still mad that he hadn't come with me while another man unpacked his bags in my room.

"The drive was as expected, long and boring. I had to slurp Starbucks to stay awake, but I made it in one piece."

For all I knew, he was with a woman as he spoke to me. I had convinced myself that there had to be another woman in the picture to placate myself. When I stepped back into the room, JD was in the shower. When he got out, I took one and we got dressed to have a late dinner. We tried a local pub restaurant that we'd passed on the way. It was in the square not too far from our hotel on the River.

I was surprised. I didn't know that there we this type of nightlife in Savannah. JD revealed that he had visited here before. We ate burgers, fries and had a few beers at dinner before we headed back to the hotel. I was exhausted from the drive. We got back to the room and had sex that night before I fell asleep wrapped in JD's arms. I hadn't slept through the night for two weeks since Mike had left for the last trip.

The next morning I got up and attended my scheduled meetings. JD told me not to worry about him, and he would occupy himself. The morning sessions seemed to drag on but by 1:30, my meetings finished up, and I was in route to the hotel. JD sat reclined on the bed, watching TV looking utterly relaxed.

"What have you been doing all day since I left?"

"I went to breakfast after you left. The hotel has a nice buffet with omelets and the works. Then I walked around to some of the shops here, but it was so early that I came back and took a nap for a while. You were on my mind all day. I have a surprise for you."

He got up off the bed, reached for his bag and pulled out a small box. "What's this?"

"Just open it," he said.

I hesitated. Expensive things came in little boxes, but surely, he had not done that. I opened the box, and a pair of silver and enamel butterfly earrings shone up at me from the wrapping. The wings shone with colors of turquoise, lavender, and pink. My eyes rose up to meet his, and he smiled broadly at me. The pride in his find spread across his face.

"I saw these and I thought of you. I notice how you seem to like butterflies."

"Thanks, JD, but I can't accept these. I mean, we shouldn't be spending this kind of money on each other."

His head tilted to the side slightly. The smile slipped from his lips.

He said, "When did we say that Mona? Not to downplay it, but they were not that expensive, and I want you to have them."

I wanted to disagree, I recognized the name of the jewelry store on the inside of the box, and it was no discount store.

I started to protest again and he came to put his finger to my lips.

"Why don't you take the earrings and wear them for me tonight when we go out. If you can't keep them you can give them back to me tomorrow."

He pressed them into my hand and I knew then that he wasn't going to take them back. That night we left the hotel to take in the nightlife of Savannah. My coworkers had all gone to a company sponsored food truck event that I decided to ditch. I also knew it lessened the danger of JD and me running into them. I wore a little pink dress with a flirty ruffle that stopped above my knees. The silver strappy wedges on my feet perfectly complemented the butterfly earrings JD gave me. We went out to a seafood place on River Street. You couldn't come to Savannah and not have seafood, mainly since it was my favorite food. The establishment wasn't fancy by any means with its cheap red and white checkered tablecloths, but the food was divine. I ordered fried soft shell crab while JD went for a combination of fried and peel n' eat shrimp. With full bellies, JD held my hand and we walked downstairs to a lounge that he said he remembered from the last time he was in the city. The crowd was a mix of many different cultures but the age group was over thirty. They played a lot of pop and some hip-hop hits from the 80's and 90's. JD was a good dancer. He didn't lack anything in the area of sex appeal as he moved his hips. A Keith Sweat song came on, and he pulled me to him with a bump and grind move like we were in a 90's music video. He bought drinks for us and even for a table of folks next to us that were talking about our dance moves. I felt free like I had not felt in years.

We took some shots and I got so relaxed that I let him kiss me up against a wall as we rested from the dancing. The corner was dark, and as I leaned back, he pressed his body against mine and ran his hand under my skirt. Before I could object, he slightly parted my legs, and his fingers slid on my wetness and into my folds. He worked his fingers back and forth, continued to move his hips as if we were dancing. My forehead rested on his chest and he propped me up. His fingers moved quicker. The orgasm snuck up on me, and I gasped. As I did, his mouth closed over mine to catch the sound. My heart beat erratically and the orgasm was followed by instant embarrassment. I looked around the room praying that no one figured out what we had been doing. He whispered in my ear, "No one was paying any attention to us." He was right; couples throughout the club explored their own hedonistic ways with little concern for us.

I looked to the left of the dance floor where a couple threw back shots of alcohol. They both grimaced at each other before slamming the glasses on the table. The man glanced up and met my eyes. Oh my god, was that Barry from home mortgages? I quickly turned my back to them and buried my face in JD's chest. It was dark, and strobe lights distorted the faces. Had he seen me letting this man make me come in this club? Was that even him? Panic stole my breath. I was scared to turn around. I grabbed JD's arm and pulled him to the side door that lead out to a patio. My heart raced as we walked across it to get to the other side of the bar to the exit. JD asked me where we were going. I ignored his question until we were back on the street mixed in the throngs of people bent on alcohol.

When I finally I told him that I thought I had seen a coworker, JD didn't share my fear.

"Baby, calm down. How well do you know that guy? Even if he saw you, so what. Would he say something to you?"

I rounded on him. "How can you be so nonchalant about this? What if he tells somebody? What if he tells my husband?"

"Come on Mona, does he know your husband?"

I stopped. "Well, no. He doesn't know him. But, that's not the point. What if they saw us-- saw you touching me that way? Oh my god, I have to face them in workshops tomorrow."

My hands covered my face. JD pulled my hands down and tried to hold them. I pulled away and walked towards the hotel. "We can't do this here JD. Someone else may be out here looking right at us." I tried to glance around without looking too obvious. The liquor made me feel light-headed, but I walked as quickly as my heels would let me. JD didn't say anything else. He let me walk ahead of him until we got inside the hotel, and I had to wait for the elevator. We rode up to the room in silence as I tried to process all of the possibilities in my head. I had let myself get too comfortable. I had allowed what I was doing to become ordinary.

As I used the key on the room door, JD pressed against me and wrapped his arms around me. I tried to pull away at first but he held me, and I calmed down. We were safe in the room by then. The panic I felt earlier started to wane. He continued to hold me, and I felt his hardness on my back. One minute I was shaking with fear and the next I felt arousal wash over me as JD kissed the side of my neck. Was it the excitement of discovery that turned me on? JD obviously got a thrill from it. I don't know how our clothes had gotten off, but somehow we ended up in the shower. He licked parts of my body while the water ran over me. My head swam from the alcohol. He was on his knees in front of me, spreading me, and putting his mouth where it felt glorious. My back was slid the wall, and my legs gave out. Before I could object, in a swift move, he stood up, wrapped my legs around his waist, and thrust himself up into my wetness. I held on for dear life as he drove into me. Somewhere in the back of my mind registered that there were no condoms in the shower but I couldn't tell him to stop. I didn't want him to stop. I screamed out my orgasm, and he yelled out soon after me. After we caught our breath, he washed and rinsed my body before carrying me to the bed.

Saturday morning when I woke up my head pounded. I drank too much and would regret it for the rest of the conference today into tomorrow. JD threw his long leg across me as if to keep me from escaping. When he woke, JD reached for me again, kissing the back of my neck and running his big hands over my stomach. This time I made sure he used protection as we made love before I rushed to meet my colleagues for breakfast at the conference center. I alternated between coffee and water as I attended two of the workshops for which I'd registered and ditched the third one where I saw Barry sitting at the conference table. I wasn't positive that it was he that I'd seen last night, but I decided not to tempt fate. I went back to the hotel and convinced JD to leave the suite so that I could take a nap before the evening festivities. I felt much better when I met up with my co-workers in the ballroom decorated and set up with blackjack and roulette tables. Many of my mostly male counterparts had brought their wives to the event themed as a Vegas Casino Night.

Barry and his wife waved and spoke to me over the roulette table, but neither of them looked at me questionably. I guess that wasn't him that I'd seen last night. No one blinked an eye at the fact that my husband wasn't there, he hardly ever made it to any company functions because he was always working. I still felt a pang of envy watching them interact and speak with the VP of our bank and his wife. I wished my husband were here to run interference for me. A crazy thought of JD walking in and standing by my side as we spoke crossed my mind. These folks probably wouldn't even know the difference; they hadn't seen Mike enough times to know him from any other Black male. After the event, I went back to JD, glad he was there to keep me company. When I walked into the room, he'd lit candles all around the room and lay there shirtless in only his boxers positioned like he was offering himself up for the taking. I fell on him and we clung to each other. I got overwhelmed with emotion as he plunged to the core of me. He took me to the edge of oblivion and then pulled back slowly.

"Do you like it Mona?"

"Yes I like it," I said.

"Tell me you like it. "

"I like it."

"Tell me, say it louder."

"I like it."

"Tell me you love it."

"I love it. Oh God, I'm about to come JD don't stop."

"You better tell me you love it then."

"I love it, I love it," I screamed.

"Tell me you love me."

"Please, let me come JD. Please..."

"Tell me you love me Mona."

"I love you."

He picked me up and plunged up into me while my legs encased his waist. His mouth locked on mine until I screamed as the orgasm rocked the both of us into oblivion.

JD slept, softly snoring in the bed with the covers thrown off. Last night he had wrapped his arms around me and possessed me until at least two in the morning. I didn't sleep much after our lovemaking, and I thought I heard him whisper as I was in that state between sleep and waking. It sounded like he'd said, "I love you Mona."

I tossed and turned. I searched the internet on my phone and started reading articles about painting on Pinterest. Articles about painting turned to articles about relationships, which then lead to articles about infidelity. I read about how most marriages didn't survive adultery, especially if the woman cheated. Did JD really love me?

Disgusted, I turned the phone off, got out of bed, and lay out on the balcony deck chair with a spare blanket over my legs. I had to get up out of that bed and get away from JD for a few minutes. I sat there and prayed even though I knew God wasn't listening to me. I prayed that he would help me find myself. I was lost. It was supposed to be my husband inside that room. He was the one that was supposed to be on this trip with me. I gazed out to the pier and spotted a few anglers setting up their before it got too crowded. A brisk breeze brushed across my face and tossed my wild hair. The dark water of Tybee beach sparkled like golden sequins as the sun rose. It should have been as peaceful as it was beautiful, but peace eluded me. My lack of sleep was something I would regret when we got on the road later that morning to make the drive back to Atlanta.

I wiped tears from my face on the corner of the blanket. Seagulls flew overhead, and the waves crashed and made natural music. Looking at the sunrise, I wished that I had my paints and brushes with me. The sky burned a deep orange and the one spot of white that was the sun peeked through. What was Mike doing right now? Was he asleep on his stomach with the T.V. on ESPN since I wasn't there to turn it off in the middle of the night? Did he miss me while he slept alone in a hotel bed? Was he even alone in his bed, or was he doing what I was doing right now, sitting somewhere filled with regret that our marriage wasn't like the romantic comedy of my dreams? Instead, it was more like the type of drama filled Lifetime movie of my childhood.

I stood up and stretched my body to get rid of the tightness in my back. Some of the soreness resulted from lying on the deck chair, some of it from the sex positions JD had twisted me over the weekend. I slid the glass door open and walked back into the bedroom. JD still slept with the covers thrown askew off his body. I looked at his chest and arms, dark brown against the stark sheets. I knew he would be warm. I dropped the blanket I carried on the floor, crawled into bed, and put my head on his chest. This is how I knew God wasn't listening to my prayers. It was because I would let JD make me feel like I wasn't alone. I would fill the emptiness with him, and I wasn't ready to repent yet.

We eventually got up and got our things together so that we could head back to Atlanta. JD talked about how much he had enjoyed himself. All I could think about on the way home was the fact that I was now just like my mother.

CHAPTER 15

AFTER OUR LITTLE rendezvous in Savannah, I went to work on Monday morning on a mission to find out if anyone had mentioned anything about me from the business trip. I knew just where to start. I picked up a file from my desk and took it across the hall to my co-worker Jimmy's office.

"Hey Jimmy here's that file I borrowed from you last week," I said. He was looking down at his cell phone kicked back in his chair, not even attempting to look busy.

"Hey Mona, thanks for bringing that back. Did you get what you needed?" he said smiling up at me. I looked at his blonde hair that was never out of place with its perfectly gelled curls.

"Yeah, I did. Now I have to get back on track after that weekend. What did you think of the workshops? I thought they were ok."

"Yes, I enjoyed myself. My partner and I had a blast at the Casino night. I noticed that your hubby was absent once again. I'm starting to think you made him up." He laughed, and I managed to conjure up a smile.

"No Jimmy, he's real. But remember I told you before that my husband travels a lot, so he manages to miss these things every time."

He swatted a hand in front of his face as if an annoying fly was buzzing around him, "Oh Mona, you know I'm just kidding. Speaking of husbands and wives, you did notice that Travis was also there without his soon to be ex-wife?"

Jimmy went on to tell me everybody's business. Travis had a new younger girlfriend, Jamie from accounting still dated Mr. Smith, the VP of marketing. I knew I had come to the right place to get all the office gossip. I didn't care about other folks business though; I wanted to know if my name had come up in the rumor mill. Since Travis didn't mention it, I was safe. He couldn't hold water, so if there was something out there about my encounter with JD, he would have used this opportunity to take a jab at me.

The trip to Savannah seemed to turn everything up a notch between JD and me. I got into the routine of seeing JD several times a week. Since the class ended, we had to find a new meeting spot. We started meeting at the Target on Moreland Avenue-- away from his job and mine. I didn't know anyone that lived in that area and neither did he.

Things in my life got back to normal, or at least I had started to treat the situation like it was ordinary. That was until one Wednesday morning a few weeks after the trip. I had to jump up from the meeting table and run to the ladies room in the middle of Mr. Baker's forecast presentation. I barely made it in the stall before my breakfast came up. I blamed the nausea on the Mexican food I had eaten the night before, but I had seen this situation on movies, and TV shows enough times to suspect something was up. I needed to get back into the meeting before Cheryl came to check on me. I would give her some excuse for me leaving out of the meeting. Maybe I could say I got a call from my dad or something. I felt dirty for even thinking of lying to her that way, but I couldn't deal with her questions then. I would handle it later, I thought. I had client accounts to close out.

A week later I walked back through Dr. Sherman's waiting room towards the exit. When I'd sat out there an hour before, I couldn't stop staring at the ankles of the woman sitting across from me. Her fat little feet strained against the side of a pair of dollar store flip-flops. She sat with her legs spread wide and she leaned back in the chair looking up at the ceiling. Her ankles were the size of my calves and looked like they were full of liquid. By the looks of the load that protruded from her midsection and rested on her lap, I would say that woman had to be a full twelve months pregnant. She looked miserable, and she made me feel miserable before the nurse called my name to go in to meet with the doctor.

As I walked back through the waiting room, I don't think I noticed not one person at all. I couldn't see, think, or hear. When I stepped out into the August heat, I couldn't find my car. Then I remembered that I had parked on the side of the building in the shade. I hit the unlock button on my keys and sat on the blazing hot leather seat. I was numb. My mind raced, thinking about clinics, Mike, JD and Cheryl and what they would all think.

Then I came to a realization. There was nothing to think about. Nobody had to know about the situation. I could quickly go to the clinic and get it taken care of without anyone's knowledge. JD hadn't planned to have a baby with me. It was supposed to be just fucking around, right? Sometimes, it seemed like he thought it was more than a fling. Maybe I lead him to feel that way. Would he try to pressure me to keep it? My thoughts zoomed back to the past. Is this how it had started with her? Had that man killed my mother because something like this had happened between them?

When I looked up again, I sat parked in my garage with no recollection of the drive home. I remained unmoving, mind racing for at least forty-five minutes. I couldn't bring myself to go into the house. I didn't belong there. I didn't belong anywhere, not in this car, not on this planet. I was going straight to hell. I wondered if my mother would be there waiting for me. The walls closed in on me. I jumped out and walked down the street towards the tennis courts. It didn't matter that the sun's flames licked over my forehead or that I wore four inch heels and a suit jacket. Nothing mattered but how I was going to get out of this mess. I pulled my phone out of my jacket pocket. I wanted to call Cheryl and tell her what was going on. She would tell me what to do, she always had a plan. I pressed her number, but then I hit end call. I didn't want her to know this about me. She'd see how stupid I was for getting myself caught up like that.

I walked until my feet hurt-- until the soles of my feet felt on fire like the black asphalt. I limped back to the house and sat on the front porch. I licked my lips and tasted salt. I swiped at my face and felt the wetness. Sweat and tears mingled together on my face, mixed with my makeup. I needed to pull myself together. I was supposed to meet up with JD immediately after work tomorrow, and then Mike would be home tomorrow night. I had to act normal. Would I be able to move like everything was typical? I guess I could if I dug down deep enough. I had lied to him all this time. What would be different about tomorrow?

CHAPTER 16

I BACKED MY CAR into the parking space. I needed to run into the store. My stomach was out of control. I hadn't been able to hold any food down. I kept my sunglasses and head wrap on as I went through the checkout line, quickly paid the cashier, and headed back out the door. As soon as I hit daylight, I cracked the top on the ginger ale bottle and turned it up to my lips. The bubbles burned my throat at first, but as the cold liquid hit my stomach, it seemed like I was already feeling relief.

When I turned the corner of the building, I saw the familiar blue motorcycle zoom up the hill towards our meeting spot. I put the top back on my drink and quickly tucked it into my backpack. JD rolled to a stop for me to get on the bike. He took his helmet off and kissed my lips. I hesitated for a minute, considering telling him to let me take my car. I didn't know if my stomach could take the bumps of the ride on the back of a bike, but I didn't want to let on that anything was different. I wasn't ready to talk yet. I could wait until I got to his place but I didn't think I'd be able to carry on our usual conversation without letting something slip. It felt as if the secrets inside me were like the bubbles in that ginger ale, ready to overflow if my emotions were shaken up even the slightest bit.

I had a feeling in the pit of my stomach that had nothing to do with the life I carried. A sense of dread overtook me as I slung my right leg over the bike. At that moment, I knew for sure that I was not going to tell JD I was pregnant. I didn't know what that meant about me, but I couldn't do it. I wanted to be able to walk away from him when this was over, and there was no doubt that this would be over at some point. I didn't want a tether to him for the next eighteen years. I would tell him I received a text from Mike informing me he was on the way home or something to cut this meet up short. Then what? When I got home, how would I face Mike? There was no way I could get away from him.

As I sat there behind him with my arms around his middle, my fingers resting on the smooth leather of his jacket while we zoomed past cars and road signs, different scenarios raced through my mind. What if I decided to keep the baby and let Mike think it was his? He would be elated. Maybe that would be the thing that finally made him get serious about finding a position in town. Would the difference in the baby's features be so evident that he would know it wasn't his child? It could take after me and cause no questions. What if something happened somewhere in the future and the child needed blood, or a donor and tests revealed that Mike wasn't the father? It would be worse then.

If I got rid of it, Mike would never know. An abortion would make this problem go away. How would I feel about it later? At my age, what if I had the abortion and was never able to conceive again? What if I experienced complications during the procedure? Guilt would eat at me for the rest of my life. I knew people that had gotten abortions, hell, Cheryl had gotten one sophomore year of college. I have never heard her speak of regrets. The difference between us was that my soul was already black enough as it was.

The bike jerked and snatched me out of my reverie. Every muscle in JD's body tensed as he tried to regain control of the bike. I tried to hold on, but my fingers slipped from his slick leather covered waist. We were going down as we went into the curve. I felt myself flying for a split second, and then I was rolling and tumbling. Then... nothing.

CHAPTER 17

WHAT IN HELL WAS that loud beeping? Was it my alarm? My eyes wouldn't open. I tried to see where the noise was coming from. There was something around my neck, choking me. I wanted to pry it off, but my arms wouldn't move. People talked and I could feel someone touching me. It had to be more than one person because they handled my arms and legs at the same time. I couldn't understand why they were trying to strangle me, I wanted to tell them to stop, and I couldn't breathe. It felt as if someone was standing on my chest. A sharp pain shot through my arm as someone lifted it. I tried to scream, but nothing came out. They were killing me. I was dying. Finally, I would see my mother again...

Oh my God-- the pain in my leg woke me up. I tried to open my eyes, and when they finally obeyed the light was so bright, I couldn't focus on anything. The pain was taking my breath. I tried to sit up, and a crushing pain ran across my chest, as I gasped for air the sharp pain intensified. I struggled to take shallow breaths. I could feel tears running down my face, but I still couldn't focus. Where was I? I remembered the beeping from before; it was still beeping. Why was I in so much pain, what had happened? The beeping got faster. I couldn't lift my arm; it felt heavy and dead against my side. Was I in a hospital?

Finally, my eyes started to focus on the fluorescent light on the ceiling. This wasn't anywhere I recognized, but it definitely had to be a hospital. I heard a click and some footsteps. A woman came and stood over me.

"Oh Mrs. Jacobs, I see that you are finally awake."

I tried to talk but nothing came out but a wheeze.

"Now relax honey. You have four broken ribs and a punctured lung. I'm sure it hurts like hell. Don't try to talk. Settle down and rest. I'm just checking your blood pressure and giving you some pain meds. Squeeze my hand if you understand. This medicine is probably going to knock you right back out now."

I felt her put her hand in mine. She had on gloves. I squeezed. It hurt.

"Now honey you were involved in a pretty bad accident. Your husband went down to the cafeteria to get something to eat. He's been here for two days straight. I'm going let the doctor know you are awake."

Did she say my husband? Had Mike been there? When had he gotten here? Had I been in a car accident or something? How long had I been out? The door clicked again as the nurse left. Did I have brain damage? Suddenly I felt sleepy. I tried to force my eyes open as they got heavy. I wanted to see Mike. He would tell me what was going on.

When my eyes opened next time, it didn't take so long to focus. The room was dim, but I saw light peeking around the shade. From the looks of it, it was either very early in the morning or almost nighttime. I realized someone was holding my left hand. I couldn't turn to see who it was so I squeezed. It still hurt to breathe. I squeezed again and felt the person jerk. Mike appeared in my vision, standing next to the bed looking down at me.

"Oh my God, Mona. How do you feel? I'm so glad you are awake. Are you in a lot of pain? Do you need the nurse?"

He was shooting questions at me like bullets from a machine gun. I was happy to see him. I think I smiled at him, but I wasn't sure. He looked worried and something else that I couldn't put my finger on. My throat felt like a sand trap.

"Wa-ter," I croaked.

He ran out of the room and came back about five minutes later with a Styrofoam cup covered with a lid with a straw poking out. He put the straw to my lip. I could barely suck anything up through it. It felt like I couldn't get enough air to take a sip. I finally got a few drops, enough to wet my tongue and my dry throat.

"W-what h-happ-ened to me?" I finally got out.

A strange look crossed Mike's face. He hesitated before saying, "You were in a motorcycle accident."

I repeated questioningly, "A motorcycle acc..." That's when it all rushed back to me-- JD trying to control the bike, me losing my grip and flying through the air. What about JD? Was he ok? Wait, I was...

Mike was talking again, but I hadn't heard what he was saying. His voice cracked, and my eyes flew to his. Tears streamed down his face.

"The doctors told me the baby survived."

I couldn't catch my breath. My chest was on fire.

"I don't even know if you knew you were... Did you know you were pregnant?"

The machine beeped faster. I wished someone would stop that damned beeping. The baby that I had been thinking of killing was alive... Where was JD? Was he somewhere in the hospital too? Did Mike know I was with him? Oh God. The baby made it, I hadn't even been sure if I wanted it but...

"The dude you were riding with didn't survive."

He had moved closer to me. He stared into my eyes, more of those damned tears streaming down his face. I felt tears spring from my eyes. What was he saying? He was just saying this to fuck me up.

"W-what?" I tried to sit up and fire shot through me. I gasped. That damned machine started going haywire. The nurse ran in and nudged Mike out of the way. My head felt like it was going to explode. Was JD really dead? I couldn't breathe at all now. I tried to look at Mike. The nurse asked him what we had been doing. They put another I.V. in my arm. Someone else came and stood over me. I assumed it was the doctor. They spoke medical jargon that I didn't understand. Someone put a mask over my face. Then it got dark.

    I startled awake when the door clicked. Mike sat in the room in a chair across from me, but he wasn't looking at me. He stared at the wall. It felt like a barbell rested on my chest, the pressure was so immense. My head throbbed. J.D was dead. Did Mike know everything? Why didn't I die? I sobbed, my body shook, and I couldn't stop it. It hurt. Mike finally turned towards me. His face was unreadable. He didn't move towards me at first. He just looked at me with a granite expression, his eyes bloodshot and expressionless.

"Why were you on a motorcycle? Who was he, Mona?"

I couldn't stop crying. I wanted Mike to hold me, but I couldn't expect that now could I? Where was my daddy?

"Mona! Do you hear me? Who was that man you were on the bike with?"

Mike had raised his voice. I had never heard that tone before. I still couldn't say anything.

"Just tell me this. Is that my baby in your belly?"

I sobbed harder and my throat burned. I closed my eyes because I couldn't look at him. They were dead --my baby and its father--my lover. Both of my secrets were secrets no more. I couldn't think about what this meant. Mike stood up and walked over to the bed. He looked down at me.

"Since you have nothing to say, that tells me what I needed to know."

He then turned his back on me and headed towards the door. I heard a loud click as he closed the door behind him. I cried until there was nothing left. Mike didn't come back. The nurse came in and out. She didn't say much, but I thought I saw a look of pity cross her face. She probably knew the whole story, and now I was a topic of gossip amongst the nurses. I just wanted her to turn the lights out and leave me alone. I wanted more drugs so that I could sleep for a very long time. That was the least she could do for me.

When I woke up again, I realized there was someone in the room with me. I didn't think Mike was back. I turned my eyes to see it was my daddy. He stared at me. When our eyes met, his he smiled, but the smile on his lips didn't reach his eyes.

"I finally caught you awake baby girl." He squeezed my hand. "Every time I've been here you never wake up." He bent down and kissed my cheek. I smelled a hint of gin on his breath. His usually shiny slick bald head had the shadow of stubble on it. He hadn't been to the barber. The wrinkles around his mouth and eyes looked like canyons. I could tell that he hadn't been sleeping. He held my hand and searched my face. I averted my eyes.

"Baby girl, I'm so glad that you're still here with me. I thought I was going to lose you."

My eyes welled up at the worry I saw on his face. I hated that I was the cause of it. My father had already felt enough pain in his life caused by a woman he'd loved. He stroked my hair as he sat beside my bed. It was hard to believe that those wrinkled brown hands that moved with such gentleness had ever taken someone's life.

"Baby, what were you doing on that motorcycle anyway? I've never known you to be riding those things. Who was your friend?"

The tears fell from my eyes. Dad wiped them away with a tissue. I didn't want to tell him. I didn't want to see the judgment on his face.

"I know that this isn't going to be a good situation baby. I was in here with Mike yesterday, and I know something isn't right. He was praying for you to wake up all day, but last night he wasn't saying anything, just standing there staring at you. I tried to talk to him, but he just kept telling me to ask you what happened."

I closed my eyes, I tried to choke something out, but only squeaky noises came from my throat.

He reached over and rested a hand on the part of my arm that was not in a cast. "You know what, that's not important right now. Just rest. I'm sorry Monie, so sorry this happened to you."

I was sorry too. Would my daddy still feel the same way if he knew the whole story? I couldn't bring myself to look at his face anymore, so I just kept my eyes closed and prayed that someone would come in soon and give me some more drugs that would make me fall asleep.

***

Cheryl sat next to my bed when I woke up. It took a minute for my eyes to focus. She was reading a Women's Health magazine. I said a scratchy, "Hey girl." She tried to smile, but I could see the worried turn of her lips. She put the magazine down on the table and grabbed my hand.

"How are you feeling today?"

I took a minute to take inventory of my body. I moved my arm and took a deep breath to see if the pain had subsided. My ribs still hurt like hell, but it was nowhere as bad as it had been two weeks ago. The doctor had said that depending on how I did over the weekend, I could probably go home Monday. That brought tears to my eyes. Would I even have a home to go to on Monday?

"Mona, what's wrong. Do you need me to call the nurse?"

I shook my head as the tears started tracing new lines down my face. I promised myself I was not going to cry like this again.

Cheryl did the best she could to hug me without hurting my ribs. It hurt a little bit, but it felt good to have somebody comfort me. I finally got my tears under control. She pulled back, and I saw that she had tears on her face too. She got us some Kleenex from the counter and wiped her own eyes before wiping mine. She sat back down in the chair and held on to my hand.

I tried to talk without my voice trembling. It didn't work.

"The doctor said that I can probably go home Monday... However, I don't have a home do I? Where am I supposed to go?"

Cheryl squeezed my hand.

"Don't worry about that. You are coming home with me. I told Ray that he was just going to have to move his weight bench out to the garage until you are well enough to go home."

I managed a laugh. "You are just so bossy. I can't impose on y'all like that. I think I just may have to stay with my daddy..."

She cut me off, "Now you know you don't want to stay over there. It's not imposing. You are my best friend and you know I would do anything for you... Even though I'm really pissed at you right now."

"Why are you mad?"

She pursed her lips at me and gave me that look that said I knew the answer to that question.

"Well, I almost had a heart attack when I heard you had been in an accident. Imagine the surprise when I found out that your baby was ok and you were with some dude that I had never heard of before."

I felt a stab of pain and guilt at her words.

"I'm sorry that your friend died Mona. I didn't mean to say it like that. But, I'm your best friend. How could you not tell me you were pregnant? Why couldn't tell me what was going on?"

I closed my eyes because I felt the tears starting again. It seemed like a person should have a limit on how much they could cry.

"I just couldn't tell you. I didn't know how to tell you because I didn't want you to judge me. I wanted blab the whole story every time I saw you, but I couldn't get the right words together. I wanted to call you so bad when I found out I was ..."

I couldn't say it. I covered my face with my right hand. The tears seeped through my fingers. My shoulders shook as I sobbed. She just sat there and held my hand.

"Mona, I'm so sorry. I didn't know what to think at first but don't you know I love you? We've been through so much together, and I've done dirt that you know about. Why would you think I would judge you? Yes, I would've told you that you were making a mistake, but I'm still your friend no matter what you do."

I wiped my tears with another tissue.

"Have you seen Mike? He hasn't been back up here since he found out... I know he won't want me back in the house."

Cheryl looked at me earnestly, "Mona, I know you probably haven't looked at it this way because you feel guilty. That is your house just as much as it's his. You did some things that were wrong, but he can't put you out. I know you don't want to face him right now. I haven't seen him around. I tried to call him, but he won't answer my calls. I wanted to know if he was ok. Ray tried to call him too thinking that maybe Mike would answer if he saw his number, but he still didn't pick up."

I sighed heavily before saying, "He doesn't want to have anything to do with me or anybody that knows me."

Cheryl stayed with me for the rest of the evening until visiting hours were over. We didn't talk much more about my situation after that. She just sat there reading her magazine and giving me the latest updates on what had been happening at work. I was thankful for her being there. I was also grateful that as a friend she knew that I didn't want to talk about painful things anymore.

CHAPTER 18

THE DOCTOR DIDN'T release me on Monday as he initially said, but by Wednesday morning, I was ready to go home. Fitted with a new sling for my left arm and dressed in white t-shirt and a pair of navy blue jogging pants that had one leg cut off to accommodate my cast, Cheryl was busy packing up the stuff that had accumulated in the hospital room. She had two big shopping bags filled with the flowers, candy, fruit, and stuffed animals that coworkers had brought me. She also made sure to go through all of the cabinets to get any gauze, tape, bandages, or anything else that she could find in the room.

When I looked at her quizzically, she stated, "When you see how much you have paid for all of this stuff on your medical bills, you will be glad I snagged it."

Cheryl signed the release paperwork for me and gathered up my prescriptions before she headed down to pull her SUV around to the patient pick up area. I waited for the tech to come back with a wheelchair to take me downstairs. I sat alone as comfortably as I could on the edge of the bed. My head snapped up when the door opened. The tech was rolling the wheelchair into the room. The shock came when I saw who was ambled in behind her. My husband walked hesitantly into the room.

Tears sprang to my eyes. I was so happy to see him, happier than I had been in a long time because of his presence. I met his gaze, and he looked away. The tech chattered on about how she bet I was glad to be going home. If only she knew. Mike helped her to get me in the chair and then hurried to snatch his hands away as if he was repulsed to be touching me. It hurt. I thought of all of the times that I had pretended to be asleep so that he wouldn't attempt to make love to me. I would never have to worry about that again.

When we got downstairs to the loading zone, Cheryl stood beside her car. Mike had pulled up behind her, so I know they had seen each other. The tech followed Mike to his car and Cheryl walked over before they could help me out of the chair. She looked at me intently.

"You know that you are still welcome to come home with me. I have your room all ready." She followed this with a pointed look at Mike.

He said in a stern but quiet voice, "She's coming home with me. I can take care of her."

The tech looked back and forth between the three of us with an expression that said she just wanted to rid herself of me and go back inside before the drama unfolded.

Finally, Cheryl stepped back in acquiescence. "I want to make sure ain't no 'Diary of a Mad Black Man' shit going to be happening over there. You aren't going to mistreat her or be holding her hostage are you?"

She was dead ass serious and didn't crack a smile. Mike gave her a look that would wither a lesser woman.

"Ok, fine. You take Mona with you, but you better take care of her, and I will be visiting every day to make sure you are," she said.

Mike moved to open the passenger door of his truck, and the tech look relieved that we had made a decision without involving the Atlanta Police Department. They got me settled in the truck with the front seat of the extended cab pushed back as far as it could go. Cheryl put the bags of my belongings behind the driver's seat along with my hospital issued crutches. She hugged me tightly and told me to call her if I needed anything at all. She also turned and gave Mike a quick hug that caught him with his arms stiff by his side, but he didn't recoil from her.

With a slight smile on her face she said, "Mike, you be sure to call Ray or me if you need us to do anything, ok. Promise me that you will do that."

Mike only nodded. We were all so drastically different from the two couples that used to go out to happy hours together and have game nights on the weekends.

The ride to our house was only twenty minutes, but the tension was so thick in the cab of the truck that I couldn't wait to get out. Mike didn't say one word to me as he maneuvered on the interstate and side streets to our neighborhood. I racked my brain, searching for something neutral to say. Everything I thought of just seemed stupid and petty considering the circumstances. Not only that, I was afraid that anything I said would cause Mike to change his mind about taking me home. I was scared that he would pull the truck over to the side of the road at any minute and roll me out into oncoming traffic. I didn't want to do anything to provoke his temper.

When we got to the house, Mike hit the button to raise the garage door but stopped short of pulling in. He got out of the truck and went through the garage into the house. He came back out rolling a collapsible wheelchair. I was surprised but didn't say anything. He scooped me out of the truck into his arms and then placed me gently into it, all without meeting my eyes. He wheeled me into the house, through the kitchen, and to the largest guest room. I never thought I'd be coming home, so the thought of where I'd sleep hadn't crossed my mind. It was obvious Mike didn't want me in our bedroom with him. Mike had rearranged the room so that it was easier to maneuver around and I noticed that he'd taken the large dresser and side chair out of the room. Once again, he scooped me up and put me into the bed, and I couldn't help but inhale his familiar scent.

Finally, after getting me settled, he said something, "I'm going to go and fill your prescriptions. Your pain medicine is going to start wearing off soon."

He didn't give me time to respond but walked out the door and closed it behind him. I didn't know what to feel. I thought of all of the things that we needed to discuss and all the bad feelings that had grown between us that were now amplified ten-fold. I sat back and tried to ignore the pain in my body or the thought that my husband seemed to have decided that he was going to take care of me. I hoped it meant all was forgiven but the rational part of me knew that was impossible. His actions that day had proved to me how much he loved me as much as my previous actions proved I had taken his love for granted.

He came back, gave me a handful of pills to take, and arranged the rest of the medication on the nightstand, all in silence. Suddenly, an image of my body lying in bed foaming at the mouth flashed in my mind. I hoped he wouldn't try to kill me with an overdose of pain medication. I probably deserved it.

Before I could think more about it, the pills made me drowsy, and I drifted off to sleep.

Someone cried out. I could hear my mother crying in the front room, but it sounded muffled. It couldn't be mama. I looked down at myself to notice the bandages and cast were gone. I climbed out of my bed and slipped my feet into the pink Strawberry Shortcake slippers that my aunt had given me for Christmas. Mama told me never walk to through the house in bare feet because the wooden floor in the hallway was so cold in the winter. I crept down the hall to mama's room. When she cried in the middle of the night, I always climbed into bed with her. It always helped her to stop crying when I snuggled up to her. When I got to her room and peered in, she wasn't there. The sheets were rumpled, so maybe she had gotten up to get something to drink from the kitchen. As I approached the living room, I heard mama crying, but I stopped in my tracks when I picked up a man's voice that wasn't my daddy's. Something in their hushed tones told me not to just run into the room where she was the way I wanted to.

I peeped around the door to the living room. Mama stood with her back against the kitchen counter. She wore the old soft yellow robe that she usually put on after getting out of the bath. Her hair hung down to her waist wild and tangled like she had just gotten up and hadn't had time to brush it. A man stood in front of her with his back to me. I recognized him; I had seen him in town before. He was a mechanic where mama took the car to get it fixed. He was wearing a black leather coat that hung to the back of his thighs. On his head rested a wool cap pulled down low over his ears as if he had just walked in out of the cold. He grabbed my mama by the arm and pulled her towards him in a hug.

The tears streamed down her paper bag colored face. She could barely speak.

"I can't come with you Rodney, I'm sorry. You have to leave. My husband might be home any minute."

"I don't care Debra. It's time that he knows about us. You said that if you had the chance, you would leave him. Well, I'm here. Here's your chance. Let's go, baby. I got you. You don't have to worry 'bout nothing."

Mama gulped in air. She tried to pull away from him, but he wouldn't let her go.

"I told you that we had to end it. I need to do right for my family."

"But you told me you loved me. We can leave for Philly tonight. You wanted this. We can talk to your husband together if you are scared, or we can just go. He will figure it out."

"Please Rodney, you can't' be here. We can't do this. Please go... I'm sorry... I can't leave my baby here. I love my family. I'm going to work it out, make things right."

"You are just saying this because you're scared, baby. I love you, and I will take care of us. Baby you don't have to stay here. I know you want to be with me. Let's go, we have to go."

Mama put her hand on his back and tried to lead him to the door. He grabbed her wrist and started walking towards me. That's when they both saw me.

Mama had a funny smile on her face when she looked at me. "Mona, go get back in the bed honey."

I couldn't say anything. I couldn't move. Mama took my hand and tried to lead me to my bedroom. He snatched her arm.

"Come on Debra, get some clothes. Where's your suitcase?"

He was pulling her down the hall. Mama looked at me.

"Mona honey, it's ok. Go back into your room and close the door ok. You can turn on your record player."

I stood frozen there, wishing my daddy would come through the door. I didn't know what to do.

Mama started trying to pull away. "No Rodney I'm not going with you. I'm staying with my family. That's why I told you we had to end it. Don't you understand?"

He snatched her arm harder. She stumbled, and her shoulder crashed into the doorjamb. She whimpered. "Rodney, you are hurting me."

His eyes got wide; the look on his face scared me.

"So what are you saying, Debra? You lied to me?"

"No Rodney, I wasn't lying, I just... I just can't leave them. I can't do this to them. I'm sorry."

He was yelling now. "Stop telling me that you're sorry... you don't mean that shit. You can't mean that shit. You're trying to tell me that you were just using me for a fucking thrill? You ain't happy here with him. Where is he now? You said you loved me, Debra."

He grabbed her and kissed her hard. Mama was trying to push him off her. I finally was able to make my feet move. I ran up the hall by my bedroom door, but I didn't go in. I was scared to leave her there. He pulled mama into her bedroom.

"Debra, why are you acting like this? Just get your things. Once we get on the road, you will feel better. I'm not going without you."

"But you have to. I'm not leaving my baby, my husband. I'm sorry that I said those things. I thought that was what I wanted, but I realized it's not the right thing. I can't abandon my daughter."

"We can bring her. I just want you with me. We don't have to leave her. Just stop talking like this."

Mama was screaming now. "Rodney, listen to me! I'm not leaving but you have to. You have to leave here before something bad happens. I can't leave with you. You just have to leave by yourself. My husband's coming home, and you can't be here... Please, Rodney..."

"I can't believe you are doing this to me. You lying bitch. What was I, just some sucka for you? You were just playing with me to make your husband mad or something, making him jealous. Were you just fucking around with me to see if you could get me caught up? I can't believe you're doing this shit to me. You were lying the whole time you were fucking me."

He was walking towards her. He reached into his pocket and pulled out a big gun. It was black and shiny like the one my daddy kept in his car. Mama put her hands up with her palms facing him as if she was trying to block the anger.

"Please, please, what are you doing? Please put that down. I wasn't lying. I do love you. I just can't go with you tonight... Please!"

She cried, and tears were on his face too. I stood there.

"I'm not going without you, Debra... I can't go without you. I love you, and you are doing this to me. I can't go without you..."

He just kept shaking his head back and forth and pointing the gun at her. Then I heard a car outside.

Gallery of Lies

"Please, Rodney, just calm down. We can talk about this tomorrow. We can figure something out. I just can't go tonight. Please, just put the gun down..."

"I can't Debra. You're lying. You ain't nothing but a lying whore. I can't leave here without you. Don't you understand that? I can't. I can't let you stay here. You said you loved me."

I heard the front door click, and my daddy's voice call out. "Debra, where you at?"

I yelled, "Daddy!"

Mama tried to run towards the door. I turned and ran towards my daddy. The next thing I heard was a loud boom. Daddy ran past me. He ran into the hallway, and there was another loud boom and then another and then another. I covered my ears, but I still heard my daddy calling mama's name over and over again.

"Debra! Debra baby, oh my God. Debra baby hold on!"

I ran into the hall and tripped over the leg of the man that mama had been arguing with. I looked, and he was slumped against the wall. The gun lay on the floor beside him. He reached a hand towards me. I scrambled back up to my feet, and when he turned to look at me, it was JD's bearded face smiling up at me. I backed away and ran to mama and daddy's bedroom. Daddy was on his knees holding mama's head in his lap. A big red spot was spreading on her chest, soaking through the yellow cloth of the robe. I stood there. She turned towards me, and I looked into my own gray eyes. Screams shrilled in the air. Someone was screaming over and over again. They kept screaming. I kept hearing the shots firing like a cannon. Why wouldn't they stop screaming?

Someone shook me. I jerked awake. Mike stood beside me calling my name. My throat felt raw. I hadn't had this nightmare in a long time. I was sobbing, and I couldn't get control of myself. Mike wiped my face with the sheet.

"Mona, Mona... It was a nightmare. It's ok."

But, it wasn't ok. It was never going to be ok. I couldn't catch my breath. I couldn't stop the tears from streaming down my face. I wrapped my arms around Mike's neck. I cried uncontrollably on his chest. He put his arms around me and stroked his big hands up and down my back. He had always comforted me when I had these nightmares a long time ago. I missed this. He suddenly snatched back from me and pulled my arms from around his neck. He cleared his throat and avoided my eyes as I searched his face for a connection. He handed me the cup of water that rested on the nightstand.

He stood up from the bed. "It was just a nightmare. Have a drink of water and try to get back to sleep."

With that, he walked out of the room without turning around. I lie back on my pillows, and this time the tears that ran down my cheeks had nothing to do with the nightmare.

CHAPTER 19

CHERYL CAME INTO the room and gave me a hug and kiss on the cheek. I was elated to see her. I had been so lonely. I wished I could go back to work; at least it would give me something to occupy my mind other than the self-loathing thoughts that played on a constant loop in my head now. I was tempted to call my boss and ask him if I could take on some work from home, but I didn't think I would be able to do much typing with my right hand yet.

She pulled a chair up to the bed beside me.

"Girl, what are you watching on T.V.?"

I hadn't even been paying attention to the episode of Real Housewives of Atlanta that played on screen.

"I wasn't looking at it. I think I have seen that episode anyway. I hate to watch it sometimes because the show doesn't portray any reality about black women in Atlanta. It's just for entertainment."

Cheryl laughed. "Girl I know that's right. They need to have some cameras following some real women around. We would give the viewers something for their asses, right?"

She snorted with laughter before she realized that I wasn't laughing with her. She finally looked at me and took my hand.

"Mona, I'm sorry. I guess that was insensitive for me to say. But actually that time I was talking about my own drama, not yours."

"Oh yeah, what drama do you have in your life right now?"

She smacked her lips. "I know you have a lot going on, so I don't want to bombard you with my bullshit. What's going on with you? How is it around here with you and Mike?"

I sighed, "I really would rather hear about your drama than talk about that. Nothing is going on with Mike and me. He takes care of me, makes sure I take my medicine, and makes sure I get in the bathroom, but that's about it. He usually doesn't have two words for me."

"I'm sorry, girl. I know that's rough. I bet he's trying to punish you any way that he can, but he loves you enough to take care of you. Maybe y'all can work it out some kind of way."

I felt myself tearing up, and I didn't want to cry today, not right now anyway. Therefore, I changed the subject back to her.

"So what's up? What's going on with you? I need a story to take my mind off this mess I'm in."

"Well... I don't know if I want to talk about this either, but I might as well. Anyway, you know how I told you Ray had been acting like an asshole for the past few months?"

"Yeah, I know you said he wasn't listening or whatever. I hope you aren't about to say what I think you are... "

"Shit honey, if you think I'm about to tell you I suspect he's cheating on me then you got it."

I sucked in a breath of surprise. "I can't believe that. Not Ray."

Cheryl turned a look on me that made me cringe and close my mouth as quickly as I had spoken. I sure was one to talk about disbelief.

She looked me in the eye. "People do things that we never expect all the time. I always thought we had the type of marriage where we would be able to talk through anything. I don't have concrete evidence or pictures of him fucking, but in my heart, I know he's doing dirt."

I shook my head. "Well maybe he is just thinking about doing it, but he hasn't done anything yet. You know what I mean?"

I didn't know what to say nor did I want to lie. Ray could have gotten himself into a situation the same way I had. However, I couldn't fathom what Cheryl would have done to force him to go to another woman. Of course, I knew that even though she was my best friend, I didn't know everything that went on behind closed doors. I'd kept secrets from her, hadn't I?

"The thing is Mona; I see all of the signs. He has started so-called working late these days. I see him sending a lot more text messages. He used to leave his phone around the house in plain sight without a care, now he never leaves it in the room with me as if he is scared I'm going to go through it. I always said I would never do anything like that. That's asking for trouble, but I've been thinking about it. I've been thinking about doing crazy shit like hiring a private investigator. It's eating me up, but I don't know if I'm prepared to find the truth. I don't know what I would do. I might murder his ass."

"Well, they say that most women know when their husbands are cheating but don't want to face it? I guess those signs do seem to point in that direction."

She closed her eyes and put a hand on her forehead as if trying to stave off a headache. I felt horrible that she was going through this.

She opened her eyes and pinned me with a questioning look. "I have wanted to ask you this. You don't have to answer if you don't want to but... What made you do it?"

I sat back. I didn't say anything for a minute. "I don't know really. It felt like a compulsion as if it was in my DNA. At least I used that excuse. I felt entitled because I was lonely and angry about shit that was happening between Mike and me. I thought I was the kind of person that if it got to the point of looking outside the relationship, I would take a stand and we would be able to work through it. When temptation showed up, I reasoned that I had told him I was unhappy and he didn't care. I suppose I did it partially to hurt him too, the way I thought he hurt me by staying away."

I could see I had Cheryl's full attention.

"I don't like saying this part, but for a little while, it felt good to have someone craving me. This man pursued me and made me feel like he had to have me. He wanted me with him all the time. Now it all seems like the reasons were so fucking ridiculous. I can see that he was just a little too possessive. I more than understand how infidelity could shatter a family, but I couldn't help myself. It's like I turned into my mother."

Cheryl was nodding as if she understood. I don't know if she did.

"Wow, your mother? You told me how she died, but you never talk about her. I thought you didn't remember her that well."

I laughed then. "I really don't Cheryl. That's what's crazy about it. It's as if I was trying to repeat history except JD died and I lived. I don't know what lead my mom to do what she did though. My dad never talks about it."

"That's deep. I saw how sad you were sometimes, but a lot of times you played it off as if it didn't matter much anymore. It would be hard for me if I were by myself as much as you were. I've never said this before, but I always wondered if Mike was the one cheating on you. I thought a man that stayed gone that much had to be doing something on the side."

I wanted to say to her that I was surprised, but I wasn't. I'd thought the same things at times.

"So why didn't you ever say anything?"

Cheryl looked at me, her eyes watering. "Because, I didn't want to put it out there. I didn't want to seem like the bitchy friend that said bad things about your marriage while mine was so terrific. I thought, surely she will come to her senses and see that something isn't right with him. I thought Mike had too much opportunity to cheat. I was self-righteous --glad my husband was at home every night, and we had a good relationship."

"So all this time, you thought Mike was a fuck up, and our relationship was garbage, yet you chose to say nothing to me about it?"

"No, it's not like that. I just thought that your marriage had problems and ours didn't. Everyone has arguments and tough times, but I thought we were fine. I don't know why Ray would cheat. I keep looking at what I've been doing. I keep searching and trying not to put all the blame on him because I know it takes two to fuck up a relationship. I want you to be honest with me, am I pushing him into the arms of another woman?"

I smirked, "Oooh no. I'm not falling for that trick. You are not about to turn on me."

She made a sound like a laugh, but her lips didn't turn up into a smile. "No girl I'm for real. I know I can be a ball buster, but he has known that about me for the past eight years. Nothing has changed. I do work a lot more and since I've been trying to get my own business going, I've been working a lot at home. But, he has never said anything. We still have sex, maybe not as much as we used to, but it's not like he's not getting any."

"Well, maybe it's not about sex. Maybe it's about attention. Is it ever really about sex?"

She didn't respond, though I could tell that she was turning things over in her mind.

"I'm not the one to give advice. I just want to tell you not to let it go or try to brush it off. Ask Ray straight up, or suggest that y'all go to counseling or something. Your marriage is too important to let this get out of hand without trying to see if you can figure it out. I wish I had worked harder. Mike took me for granted, so I felt that gave me a pass to break my vows. It didn't."

She took my hand and squeezed it. "I am going to confront Ray. I just don't want to face it right now. I just want to pretend that everything is ok and hope it goes away. I'm so busy, and the business is taking off. I don't want to deal with this shit."

I saw tears well up in her eyes. Cheryl hardly ever cried. She stood up out of the chair and started fussing with the medicine bottles on the nightstand. She had her back turned to me, and I could tell she was pulling herself together, so I didn't say anything. When she turned back around, she had her spine straight and eyes clear. It was on the tip of my tongue to say that their problems weren't going to disappear, but she got it. I knew it was time to move on.

"So when are you going to get that cast off your arm?"

I was glad to change the topic of conversation. I refused to become the spokesperson for cheating spouses. Seeing Cheryl go through emotional turmoil made me feel like the scum of the earth. I wasn't prepared to hear what Mike would say to me if we ever had that conversation. That was our problem, neither one of us had wanted to deal with our shit. We were going to have to deal with it whether we wanted to or not and it needed to happen soon.

CHAPTER 20

IT HAD BEEN SIX weeks that I'd been home from the hospital. My doctor had removed the cast from my leg and replaced it with a brace. I could walk short distances with crutches. Mike no longer had to come in to help me to the bathroom. He must not have gone back to work from his FMLA leave because I heard him come in the house through the back door every night around two a.m. He'd stopped coming in my room at all. Mike filled my prescriptions and left them on the counter in the kitchen where I could find them when I went to eat. He always left me food in the fridge or soup on the stove, but he never stayed in the house while I was awake.

I knew I didn't have the right to be, but I was so angry with him for completely ignoring me. I waited each day for the hammer to drop and for him to come in and tell me that he had filed for divorce or something. I ached for him to show up and at least scream at me, curse me out, and call me out my name for what I had done. This state of unknowing was far worse than anything he could say to me. It felt like I was sitting at the bottom of the ocean and holding my breath, waiting to drown.

I decided to do something to get his attention. I sat on the sofa in the den pretending to watch bad movies on Cinemax. I watched the time on my cell phone, and as it got later, I resolved that I wouldn't cower in my bedroom this time. When he walked through the door, I would be sitting right there where he wouldn't have a choice but to face me.

I parked my butt there on the couch feeling like a zombie until finally, at 2:17 A.M., I heard the garage door go up, and his truck pull in, but the back door didn't open for what seemed like another thirty minutes. I imagined him sitting there with his head resting on the steering wheel filled with dread at the thought of entering this house with me in it. He'd probably seen the light from side lamp through the curtains when he pulled up to the house. I should have turned the T.V. and lights off, but I hadn't thought that far ahead. I clicked the television off with the remote and sat there in the dark, refusing to get up. I had dozed off by the time the click of his key in the door locks woke me. I snatched my head up too quickly and felt a pain shoot down my shoulder. I'm sure I had a grimace on my face when he walked in. The look on his face told me that he was surprised to see me sitting there. He put his head down and tried to keep walking, but I wouldn't him act as if I wasn't there.

"Mike you see me sitting here. I was waiting for you to come in."

He didn't say anything but paused and looked down at the floor.

"You can't keep acting like I'm not even here."

Still, he said nothing.

"Mike... please... just... at least look me in the face!"

He raised his eyes to mine, and it made me pause. The look of disgust he aimed at me pierced my chest like an arrow. Maybe this hadn't been a good idea.

"What Mona? What is it? I'm looking at you, now what? What do you have to say?"

"Mike, I'm... I'm sorry. I have wanted to apologize to you, but you haven't given me a chance. You won't even stay in the room long enough for me to say anything."

He held up a hand. "Mona, I don't want your fucking apology. You aren't sorry, you are only sorry that your lying, cheating ass got caught."

He didn't yell but spoke in a monotone that I knew meant that he was seething. Mike had only shown this level of anger two other times since I had known him, and neither time was it directed at me. I stumbled over words, searching for the ones that would make him hear me. I knew I didn't deserve his forgiveness, but he'd brought me home from the hospital. He hadn't talked to me, but he had taken care of me.

Tears started to run down my face. I tried to wipe them away because I didn't want to cry. I didn't want him to think I was just using tears get his sympathy or pity. I wiped them away with the tips of my fingers the best I could. I started to speak, but nothing coherent left my mouth. I cleared my throat, and he just stood there staring at me.

"Mike..." I started. "It wasn't like that. I didn't want to be with him..."

He turned around and started to walk out of the room. I jumped up to go after him, but my knee buckled under me and I went down. I reached for the coffee table to break my fall and cracked elbow against the sharp corner. It really fucking hurt like my pride. The tears fell then and wouldn't stop. I tried to rub the pain away.

I squeezed my eyes shut, hoping that when I opened them the look on his face would be different. When I finally opened them, he stood over me holding his phone in my face. I tried to back up, but my arms weren't cooperating. I know he wasn't going to hit me, was he?

He spat words at me. "Oh, is that right Mona? You didn't want to be with him. That's not what it fucking looks like."

I shook my head as he tapped the screen of his phone and a video came up on display. At first, in confusion, I couldn't make out what was happening until the picture came more into focus on the small screen. My bewilderment cleared once I recognized a familiar form with his back to the camera. It was JD standing up, moving his hips back and forth in an unmistakable rhythm.

My breathing stopped as I heard my own voice coming from the speaker on the phone. I couldn't believe what I saw. I didn't want to watch this, but my eyes couldn't turn away. It was like what the bystanders and rubberneckers must have seen on the highway during my own accident. I couldn't look away from the tragedy in progress. On screen, I moaned as JD asked me all types of erotic questions. He asked me if I loved him and I screamed yes on a throaty moan. JD then pulled me up into his arms, and you could clearly see my face over his shoulder as he picked me up with my legs wrapped around his waist.

When had this been recorded? This was in the hotel in Savannah. At first, I was afraid to look up into Mike's eyes, but then I could feel anger start to come over me. I tried to snatch the phone from Mike's hand, but he moved too fast.

"What is that? How did you get that? Were you having me followed or something?"

Mike put a hand up to his chest and started laughing. "Oh, is that all you can say? No, I wasn't having your ass followed because I trusted you, Mona. No! Obviously, your boyfriend recorded you. Was that your thing? You couldn't get enough so you had to make videos that you could watch later? And you want to know how I got it?

The muthafucka sent it to my work email Mona. I got this from some strange email address weeks ago, but I just saw it last night because it went into the spam folder. Little did I know my wife was a fucking porn star." All humor left his face.

"And do you know what the message said? It said 'She really wants to be with me.'"

My mind dashed back over memories, attempting to put pieces together. While I attended meetings at the Savannah conference, JD must have been real busy setting up some kind of hidden video production. I couldn't believe this shit. I couldn't look at Mike's face as the video stopped. It had been less than a minute long, but it felt like I'd watched a full-length feature film.

My hand involuntarily came up to my chest. I couldn't catch my breath. JD had recorded us like some sick reality TV show.

Mike snarled, "I'm guessing by that look on your face that you had no clue he filmed this." He leaned down into my face.

"Do you know how hard it is for me not to choke the life out of you after watching you getting fucked by some other dude?"

The rage in his eyes turned to the type of desperate hurt that scared me more than anything else I had ever seen in him. The murderous look he held wasn't unfamiliar though; I saw it in my nightmares every time I dreamed of my mother bleeding through her yellow robe.

"Mike, I'm sorry that you had to see that. I didn't know that I was being recorded... "

"What does it matter if you knew you were being taped? Is it supposed to make it better that you didn't know? I wanted to give you a pass and listen to your reasons, but from looking at this, it's obvious that you were in love with this dude..."

He looked up at the ceiling like he was searching for divine intervention.

"I've been going over and over it in my head Mona, telling myself that I need to be strong and deal with this like a man. Do you know what most men would have done? They would've left your ass to rot in that hospital after they found out you were out riding around with another man, disrespecting me in front of everybody in Atlanta. I feel like a sucka for bringing you home, but I did it anyway. I have so much shit on my mind that I been dealing with, there's only so much that I can take. I guess this is me getting punished for my shit. It's all coming back on me now."

"Wait, Mike. Wait, what are you talking about, being punished?"

"It doesn't even matter Mona. I'm done with this shit."

With that, he turned his back on me again.

"Mike, don't go. Please talk to me. Let's just hash it out here and now. I don't know if I can handle it, but we need to talk about how this could happen to us. I hate myself for doing this to you, for being like my mother."

I hoped that he would turn around and face me. If he did, maybe that meant we had a small chance of moving beyond this. He didn't turn though. He put one foot in front of the other and put distance between us. This time he really did walk out. The tears choked me up again. I tried once again to get up and couldn't get any leverage on the table to pull myself up. He never did turn back around.

I just lie there wishing my body were the only thing that was broken. What had I done? What had JD been trying to do by sending that video to Mike? The images flashed through my mind all night: Mike holding the video up to my face JD and my image caught up in dirty sex like a hooker. I hadn't loved JD – I knew that now. Nevertheless, I'd lusted for him. On the video, I looked like I was having the best sex of my life. I couldn't begin to imagine how Mike felt seeing his wife embroiled with another man. From the video, even I couldn't tell that I hadn't loved JD. I knew one thing; it didn't look like I loved my husband.

I lay there all night between the sofa and coffee table, trying to figure what to do next before I finally fell asleep with my cheek on the coarse fibers of the area rug.

CHAPTER 21

CHERYL PACED BACK and forth in the small area between the kitchen island and the stove.

"He must have been crazy Mona? You didn't see any signs that this dude may have been a little unstable?"

I shook my head. "No Cheryl, I never thought JD was crazy. Not like that..."

She turned to me. "What do you mean not like that? So you are saying you saw some signs?"

I looked away. "Well, sometimes he would ask a whole bunch of questions about Mike and our relationship. He would ask me why I was still with him."

Cheryl sat down at the island now and gulped the wine in her glass.

"This wine is good. I'm sorry you can't have any..."

I shot her an evil look. "A good friend wouldn't drink in front of my face."

Her lips pursed up to one side. "Don't even go there talking about what good friends would and wouldn't do. I'm just saying."

Chagrined, I closed my mouth.

"JD was an intense dude. When I was with him, I was the only one that existed. I don't even know what he had going on in his life because I didn't ask too many questions. My thought was that I didn't want to get too involved. What a joke right? He, on the other hand, was always so interested in everything I did though. That's probably why it was so easy for to me like him."

"He told me he loved once. He held me as we lay there spooning after, well you know. I pretended to be asleep so I wouldn't have to face him and say something back. I knew then that I didn't love him, but I ignored it because I didn't want to stop."

Cheryl took a sip and said, "Well, girl, I don't know how much information he had on you, but we now know he was doing enough investigation to get Mike's email address. I wonder what he was planning. It seems like he wanted to break up your marriage. I'm not taking Mike's side, but how could he watch that video and continue to take care of you? I would've tried to poison your ass."

I squirmed in my seat a little bit, but I could only laugh.

"You don't know how many times I've thought about that. I'm glad I can make my own meals now."

The conversation trailed off a bit as we thought of the heaviness of what we'd said. We both sipped on our drinks, Cheryl on the last of the wine and me on sparkling water.

"Cheryl, I have a favor to ask."

"Sure, what's up?"

"Well... can you take me to a doctor's appointment on Monday?"

"Oh, yeah girl. I can drop you off on my way to work. You can call me when your appointment is over, and I can dip out to pick you up since it's right around the corner from the office."

She thought I was talking about my orthopedic specialist. "No, not Dr. Jones. I need to go to my Ob/Gyn."

I snuck a glance over at her under my lashes. I saw that she was looking down, but she wasn't looking at me. She was biting her lower lip.

"Ok. So, just let me know what time and I will fit it in."

Cheryl didn't say anything for a minute. Trying to be quiet was killing her. She was going to chew her damn lip off.

"My appointment is at nine o'clock."

She said ok. I waited.

"Soooo... What um have you decided to do?"

Finally. I looked directly at her. "I don't know Cheryl... I don't know what to do now. On the day of the accident, I had decided to get rid of this baby just because I didn't want to get caught. Now I don't have to worry about that. My marriage is already fucked up. I was worried about Mike leaving me if he found out, or JD being stuck in my life because we'd have a kid together. What's the outcome now? Either way, I would be a single mother if I do decide to keep it. Choosing to be with JD was never an option for me, but now it would never be a possibility... He's gone. Now, I'm sure Mike and I are headed for divorce."

Cheryl leaned over and grabbed my hand.

"Well, at least now you can go with what your heart is telling you to do. Everything is out in the open, and you might as well think about what Mona wants. It's not about proving a point or hiding anything. How do you feel about being a single mother? I know it was never in your plan to raise a child alone."

I had to decide. There was no way in hell now that Mike was going to forgive me after that video. Cheryl was right. I had to look out for myself. It was time for me to review my finances in case I needed to find a place to live on my own.

***

Early Monday morning I sat in the cold, clinical gray room trying to keep my nerves at bay. This room, unlike the others, held no anatomy of pregnancy or stages of labor posters. Maybe this room with its ultrasound machine was a place of good or bad news depending on what showed on the screen or the parent's state of mind.

I lie back on the exam table while the ultrasound technician moved the instrument around on my stomach. Cheryl stood there over my left shoulder looking up at the screen as she showed us the little alien that had taken up residence in my body. As she showed us the image, first I was amazed that they had 3-D imaging. Then I was amazed even more by seeing a little face that had my daddy's nose. I smiled, and tears instantly came to my eyes. I looked over at Cheryl, and she was smudging the corner of her eyeliner with her pinky finger as well.

I knew then what I was going to do. Here was my little miracle. We should have both died in that accident. This baby was a survivor and so was its mommy. I had to keep this baby no matter what would happen and pray that things would work out.

CHAPTER 22

IT HAD TAKEN A FEW months but I finally settled into the idea of motherhood. The mirror revealed my growing baby bump. I stood there at times, staring at my belly, running my hand over it. The doorbell rang, and I assumed Mike answered it because I heard the door open and close. Then I heard the gravelly voice of my father greeting Mike. It was a brief greeting, and I didn't even hear Mike's response. He had better not be giving my daddy the cold shoulder. It was only a few minutes before daddy came into my room.

"Hey, Monie," he said as he leaned over my bed to hug me.

"Mike said he was heading out to the store... Are y'all ok? He was acting like he couldn't get out of here fast enough when he saw it was me at the door."

I wanted to smile and say yes, but I couldn't make it happen. He pulled the only chair in the room closer to the bed and grimaced as he bent down to take a seat in it.

"Is your back bothering you, Daddy?"

"Yeah, it's supposed to rain today. You know my back stiffens up when the weather changes. How are you feeling?"

I didn't want to tell him that I suffered with horrible morning sickness every day and puked my guts out in a bucket by the bed so that I wouldn't have to hobble to the restroom.

"I'm doing as well as expected I guess."

"Well, I guess that's all you can ask for right now."

I looked him over like I always did. He looked better today. His head looked smooth and moisturized. He wore one of his favorite shirts. It was a white Stacy Adams shirt with wide black stripes down the center front. He must have been to the barber this morning. Most importantly, all I smelled on him was the Cool Water cologne that he favored.

"Daddy you're looking good. You must have finally decided to try to impressMs. Bea from the church?"

"See, there you go. I'm not trying to impress anybody. This is my lucky chess shirt. I was playing against Omar up at the shop. I finally won the game we had going for three weeks."

I managed to smile at that. I was glad daddy was getting back to his normal routine after knowing I was going to be ok. I wondered if he had been to a meeting.

"Well, I'm glad you won. Have you been taking your medicine?"

That must have been the wrong thing to say right then because he used his firm voice with me.

"I'm over here to check on you and you asking me questions. I'm not the one laid up in a leg brace."

His eyes held mine, and he grabbed my hand. I looked away first, pretending to need to shift in the bed.

"Monie, I've been so worried about you. I have always been worried about you. You remind me of your mother so much. I tried so hard to keep you from going down the wrong path."

I sighed.

"I'm just going to ask you straight out? Do you know for sure whose baby that is?"

My heart sped up the same way it had when I was a teenager, and I got caught trying to sneak out of the house after curfew. I didn't want to talk about this with my daddy. What did it matter now whose baby this was? I was going to be alone either way. I desperately scrambled for a way to change the subject.

"Daddy, I... I don't know... I don't want to talk about this."

He was shaking his head slowly back and forth with his eyes were squeezed shut.

"I don't understand why you would do something like this. You know this is the exact thing that messed up our lives. I always knew you were just like her."

I couldn't get control of my breathing then. I felt blood rush up into my face.

"Daddy don't go there."

He let my hand go. "I tried so hard to teach you right from wrong. And you go out acting like a..."

I cut him off.

"Like a what daddy?" My hands clenched. "Like a whore? Like the slut that my mama was? Is that what you were about to say? You always told me since I could remember that I was just like her. You always accused me of being fast with the boys. So I'm just like her right. I'm a slut right!"

"Now Mona, don't you get beside yourself. You don't talk to me like that. You respect me. Why were you out there running around with another man and you got a husband? I didn't teach you that. You should have known not to get involved in something like that. Look at what happened to your mama."

"What did happen to my mama? We never talked about it. I only know the pieces of hushed discussions you had with Aunt Deborah. You never sat down with me and talked to me about it."

"What do you mean Mona? You were there. You know what happened. You know that man came into our house..."

"Yeah daddy, I know that part. I still have nightmares about that night. But I was so young, too young to understand. How did it come to that? I don't know what was going on between the two of you. Why did she do what she did? What did you do? I was four years old, and all I know is that mama was acting like a slut, that's why she got killed."

He stood up out of the chair much faster than he had sat down. "Don't you talk about your mama that way!"

I jerked. He stood there shaking. I hadn't seen him this upset in a long time. I hated myself for making him this upset, but I needed to understand.

"Daddy, please calm down. Sit down. Please."

I could see his chest rising and falling. My voice calmed.

"Well tell me the right way to think about her. You never talk about her. It takes two people to ruin a marriage doesn't it daddy? Can't you at least admit that? I know I was wrong, but Mike isn't blameless is he? Were you blameless? I thought you of all people would be able to help me understand. Just tell me how to fix this."

He rubbed a wrinkled hand over his face. When his hand dropped, it looked like he had aged ten years. He didn't sit but stood there looking down at me.

I could hardly hear his voice as he spoke. "Mona, all I know is that you're lucky you aren't dead along with that man you were with. You're lucky that your husband brought you home. You need to get on your knees and thank God that he's still here with you and beg your husband for forgiveness. Unfortunately, Mona, I can't tell you what to do because I never got a second chance with your mama."

With that, he turned and walked out of my room.

CHAPTER 23

THE REFLECTION IN the mirror could not be denied. I turned to the side and tried to tug my jacket closed. My shirt looked like it was holding on for dear life as my chest and belly strained against the fabric. It was official, I could no longer hide that I was pregnant. I had seen a trick to make pants fit better by putting a rubber band around the button. It had worked for a few weeks but I was going to have to go somewhere after work to buy some maternity pants.

I searched back through my closet and found some black yoga pants. I pulled them on and found a black extra-long stretchy tank top. In the back of my closet was a blue cardigan that someone had given me some years ago that had been slightly too big. With some black pumps it looked like an intentional outfit. I didn't really look pregnant but like I had eaten a few too many orders of fries.

By the time I got to my desk this baby had already zapped all of my energy. Plus I had been limiting myself to one cup of coffee per day and had decided to save it until after lunch when the struggle to stay awake was all the way real. Before I could settle into my chair good, Jimmy popped his head into my office.

"Hey Mona, I heard you were back. How are you feeling?"

I fake smiled. "Hi Jimmy. I'm good so far. How's everything going?"

Evidently that was an invitation to come in and sit down because he did just that. "I'm sorry I never made it over to visit you. Things have been so hectic, but you got my fruit basket right? Anyway, it's good you're back. Ben has been complaining about handling your accounts and telling people that your work wasn't organized."

"Oh is that right?" Ben handled half the number accounts that I handled so I'm sure he was struggling with having to do work for a change.

"Well, I'm back so Ben doesn't have to worry about that anymore. Maybe he just had a little difficulty with understanding how to manage that number of large accounts since his are much smaller."

I hoped he'd go and tell Ben what I said. I tried not to complain about my workload because I didn't want it to seem like I couldn't handle it. But I was the only Black account manager in this region and I had twice as many accounts as everyone else. I wish Ben would say something sideways to me. I'm a professional, but with my hormones raging he just might get bitch slapped.

Jimmy laughed. "And what's been going on with Cheryl? I know y'all are besties. Why has she been looking so tired lately? And she has been late for like three meetings. You had better talk to her before she gets in trouble."

I didn't know Cheryl had been coming in late. If Jimmy was telling me that meant he had told the whole office. I had better tell her to watch herself.

"Has she been late? I hadn't noticed."

"Oh yeah, well I know you have your own stuff to worry about. I figure it must be stressful coming back after such a bad accident. But I'm glad to see you aren't too sad. I know most depressed people have no appetite and you look like you have been eating just fine."

Oh hell, did this boy just throw shade about my weight?

"Well Jimmy, I need to get back to work. I have to prepare a report for Dan. Plus, I need to work on getting all of my accounts organized so I'm going to have to kick you out."

He stood up but didn't leave. "Oh sure, I will let you get to it. But have you heard about Lisa over in claims? I heard her husband left her. That's why she been wearing all of those tight dresses, trying to catch a new man."

I used a leg to turn my chair around so that I faced my computer effectively giving Jimmy my back. "Bye, Jimmy. I'm not gossiping with you today. Plus you will be talking about me next."

I threw up a hand over my shoulder. Out of the corner of my eye I saw him finally walk out. When I turned to look he was going into Carla's office. No doubt to ask her about Lisa and probably to tell her that I looked pregnant.

I wanted to kick his ass. I turned back around and saw Cheryl coming down the hall headed towards my office. She sat down in the same chair Jimmy had just vacated.

"Girl what was Jimmy in here gossiping about now?"

My eyebrow went up. "Actually he was asking about you."

She looked towards the door. "What in the hell is he asking about me for?"

"He asked me what was up with you and said you were late to three meetings. You know if he told me that he's telling everybody in the office."

"He's such a bitch."

"Well?"

She turned back towards me. "Well what?"

"Are you going to tell me what's been happening?"

She stood and closed my office door.

"First of all, I wasn't late to three meetings, it was two and I was only like five minutes late. I know, I know, I know we can't afford to be late. But Ray's been driving me nuts. It's like we get into an argument every time I ask him about something. We had been arguing both mornings that I was late."

I leaned forward. "What is going on? Is this still about the car or did you finally ask about the cheating?"

"No girl, I haven't said anything about that. I took a peek at the books for his mechanic shop. He is in the red over there. He's been losing money and taking money out of our personal savings to cover his guys' pay checks which makes the car purchase even more perplexing."

"So why aren't you helping him?"

"You know he always says I'm so overbearing. So I tried to keep our personal life separate from the business. He had hired an accountant, but he fired the guy. He told me he could handle it himself. I don't know why, you know how jacked up his credit was when we met. I helped him get all that straightened out. It's a damn shame to be messed up financially when your wife is an accountant."

She went on to tell me that the shop had been bleeding money since he had bought the building at the new location. It had two suites for tenants but the small businesses that had rented the space hadn't stayed in business long.

"You know I have my consulting business and I wanted to expand. It looks like I'm going to have to hold off on my stuff to fix his. Then when I say something, he acts like I'm the one to blame. I think he's jealous that my business has been really gaining momentum."

CHAPTER 24

I SWIPED MY FINGER across the screen of my iPad and selected a picture of a cheery pink and yellow themed baby girl's room to add to my Pinterest "Baby Room Ideas" board. Since I decided on single motherhood, I had started to plan what the baby's room would look like. Thinking of nursery design was more comfortable than thinking about where we would live once the baby was here. I hadn't started looking for a place, and I still had not had any reasonable discussion of substance with Mike about the status of our marriage... or who would move out of the house. Cheryl kept insisting that I push for him to relocate, but how could I add that insult to the injury that I had already caused? I could see her point though; it would be easier for him to move as a single man without a baby to look after.

I got up from the edge of the bed and stood in front of the full-length mirror. I pulled my shirt up over my belly. The look of the baby bump astounded me, I couldn't get enough of looking at it, wondering what the baby was doing in there.

Mike opened and closed the door from the garage softly as if he was attempting to sneak in. I yanked my shirt back down and sat back on the bed. Mike's footsteps clicked on the hardwood as he walked down the hall. I expected him to walk past this room and head to the bedroom that we used to share like he did every day. I picked up my iPad and looked down at it intently waiting for him to pass by. The sound of the steps stopped. I raised my eyes without raising my head and saw the brown boots that he wore to work in the doorway of the room. I didn't lift my head but looked more intently at the images on the screen and even swiped my finger. Maybe this was it. The time had come for us to go toe to toe and get it all out.

He stepped into the room and said my name.

"Mona..."

I finally looked up. "Yeah." I tried not to react, but his face looked like someone had died.

"What's wrong?" I said. I started to stand up but sat back down.

"I have something to tell you."

"Oh my god. What happened, is it my dad?"

He thrust a hand out. "Oh no, no. It's not Clarence. No, he's fine."

I exhaled, and my hand went to my chest. He had almost given me a condition. Knowing that it wasn't my father had my emotions skyrocketing and then plummeting to crash.

"Ok Mike, well what is it that has you coming in here to talk to me. Can we finally talk about where we stand?"

"It's still hard for me to face you even now."

I sighed. This discussion was hopeless. "Well, you don't have to worry about that too much longer. I am going to find somewhere else to live soon."

He drew back. "I didn't ask you to move out..."

I cut him off. "Stop it, Mike. You didn't ask me to move out, but you can't even stand to stay in the same room with me for longer than a few minutes. I still can't understand for the life of me why you came and got me from the hospital if you hate me so much. Was it to punish me?"

"I came and got you because you are my wife and I promised sickness and health."

"Oh, so you can stress how you have upheld our vows even though I broke them. You don't have to rub it in my face. I feel bad every day about what I did. I know I was wrong."

He stepped into the room, closer to me. I wanted to run.

"You aren't the only one who has broken vows, Mona. This situation is all my fault, all of this. That's why I haven't been able to face you. I know that I pushed you towards that man. I pushed you to have his baby instead of mine."

I froze.

"What are you talking about Mike? What are you trying to tell me?"

My heart was beating like a tribal drum at this point. I know he wasn't going to tell me that he had cheated on me first. That would explain all the trips and weeks away from home.

He hunched his shoulders and looked away from me.

"What are you trying to tell me, Mike? Just say it."

I trembled uncontrollably as the rising anger pushed my voice up a few decibels.

"Say it!"

He turned towards me slowly. His eyes were red.

"I have a son."

I came to my feet now.

"You have a son? What do you mean you have a son? You cheated on me?"

"No, Mona... He's fourteen."

"He's fourteen? Wait, what you're telling me is that you have a 14-year-old son that you hid from me all this time? How? Why? I don't understand. "

"I... I didn't find out about him until two years ago. He lives in Arizona. I've been going out there to see him."

"And you didn't think you should tell me this for two years? I suppose all of those visits included some alone time with his mother too."

"No, no. She is married. Well, I guess that doesn't mean anything, but... "

I shot him a look. Oh no he didn't...

"I mean, it's not like that."

He sat in the chair beside the dresser.

"I knew her before I met you. I met her on campus. She and I messed around, but that was it. We were cut buddies you know, fuck friends. We never even went on a date. It was only sex between her and me. I didn't have any feelings in it. When I met you, I stopped calling her. But, not too long after you and I started dating seriously, she told me she was pregnant. I didn't want to tell you about it because I already knew I loved you. I didn't want to lose you. So, I gave her money to get an abortion and thought it was over. Obviously, she didn't get rid of the baby. I'm not proud of telling her to do that now, but back then, that seemed like the easiest way to solve what I saw as a massive problem."

"How do you know this is your kid?"

"We did a DNA test."

"And you went through all this and never thought to tell me. Your story isn't adding up Mike. Why wouldn't you tell me about this when you found out? Who is this woman?"

"Well, that's one of the reasons I couldn't tell you."

I sat up straighter.

"What? Is it somebody I know? Who is she?"

He looked down at the floor, and when his words came out, I could barely hear him.

"It's Tonya Gordon. Well, her name is Tonya Randall now."

I leaned forward.

"Who did you say? Did you say Tonya Gordon? That whore that worked at the bank when I was an intern. You swore me up and down that you two didn't have anything going on. Everybody at the bank and on the campus was fucking her. She was a stripper up at the Bombay club and as I heard it, selling ass along with the dances."

"I know that Mona. That's why I lied to you. I got caught up in a situation, and I didn't want somebody like her to break us up."

I rubbed my forehead. It was hot in here.

"I can't believe you messed with her. It's no wonder she was a bitch to me the entire time I worked in the bank. I knew something was up, I just knew it. Women don't act like that for no reason."

He squirmed in the chair, clasping his hands together as if in prayer.

"Keeping this from you has been making me sick for two years. I thought you would leave me, and I was scared. Every time I wanted to tell you, it never seemed like the right time. Then I thought if we had a child together you wouldn't be able to leave me."

I was confounded. Of all people, I never suspected that Mike could lie like that. I thought he was the good one in this relationship. I was the damaged one capable of the lies. I tasted salt on my lips and swiped at my eyes. Weren't we two peas in a fucked up pod?

Words continued to tumble from his mouth. "See, Mona, I brought you home and took care of you because I knew this was all my fault. Watching that video ripped my guts out... but I've thought about it hard. We can forgive each other and start over."

"You just thought that two wrongs were going to make a right? So when I was begging you to get a job to stay home more, you were off in Arizona with your long lost son? Not to mention that for weeks Mike you have refused to talk to me."

"I know Mona. I was humiliated and hurt when I found out about you and that dude. I've been punishing you, I admit that. But in the past couple of weeks I have started to see things differently. I know you wanted me home more. In fact, I had received an offer for a different job that would keep me home every day, but I found out about my son before I could start. So I declined the offer. I thought I would keep working in my current position a little longer, so I would have the opportunity to meet him and get to know him while I was in Arizona for work. Time flew by, and the longer I waited to tell you, the harder it got. I could feel you pulling away from me but I didn't know how to stop it. And then all of this happened."

He flailed his arms out like he was drowning. Tears fell from his eyes then. It felt like someone was squeezing my heart in a tight fist. I didn't want to see his tears. I didn't want this to be happening. Is this how he felt when he found out about my lies while I was in the hospital? Complete and utter betrayal was all I felt. I sat there facing my enemy.

I wanted to yell and scream at him, but the words that came out of my mouth were a raspy whisper.

"Get out of here."

He reached for me, and I jerked back. If he touched me, I would scratch his eyes out. I would try to put my hands around his throat and choke the life out of him.

"Get out. Get out of here."

He didn't move but sat there uttering something that I couldn't hear because of the rushing sound in my ears. My throat was raw.

"Get out! Get out!" I screamed at the top of my lungs.

He stood up. "OK Mona, please stop screaming. We need to talk this out calmly."

I ran at him and started pounding on any part of his body that I could reach. He wrapped his arms around me to keep me from hurting him or maybe, myself. I struggled until I had no more energy. Then I pushed him off of me. He backed away with his hands up in surrender.

"I will leave. I know this is a lot to process."

I turned around, picked up a book from the dresser, and hurled it at him. I missed, and it hit the wall, leaving a small dent in the sheetrock. He ducked out of the room, and a few minutes later I heard the door to the garage open and close. I slid down to the floor and rested my face on the side of the bed. How could he have kept something as crucial as a child from me? How could two people that had loved each other so much, hurt each other this much? No relationship on earth could come back from everything that happened in ours. In my mind, I settled all the questions about who would move out. He couldn't come back to live here.

CHAPTER 25

CHERYL SAT ACROSS the table from me open-mouthed holding a glass of soda and not drinking. All she kept saying was "Wow." She stood up, reached in my pantry, and pulled out a bag of chips. I shot her a look.

"What? I need chips to process all of this." She sat back down, stuck her hand in the bag, and put a chip in her mouth crunching loudly.

"Don't you want a bowl to put those in?"

"Girl no, I'll probably finish these off. But, I can't believe Mike has been hiding this from you all this time. You think you know people. Well, then again I have been getting surprised by folks keeping things to themselves lately... "

"Ok did you have to take a dig at me? I can't take another low blow."

"Sorry girl... I'm just saying. I would've never dreamed the events that happened in the past few months would ever go down like this. I understand that you never know what's going on in somebody's marriage, but damn."

I shrugged. "Yeah, imagine how shocked I am. I can't explain to you how betrayed I feel. I keep thinking about all the times I tried to talk to him, to get him to listen to me. He wouldn't cut me any slack. He wouldn't accept my apology for what happened. He shut me out completely. I thought it out of character for him, but I believed I had hurt him so badly that he couldn't face me. To discover that he was hiding this huge, no, gargantuan secret. The nerve of him to have treated me like I didn't deserve to tell my side of the story."

Cheryl nodded her head and crunched on chips as fast as she could shovel them in her mouth. I reached over and snatched the bag out of her hand.

"Stop it, Cheryl. You are going to regret it if I let you continue to inhale that whole bag of chips. You are skipping carbs remember. I don't want you blaming your wide hips on me next week."

"This story calls for a bottle of wine. I settled for chips since you can't drink. I didn't want to be inconsiderate, but if you insist. Everyone needs a vice at a time like this." My friend reached behind her and pulled a bottle out of the small wine rack. "Anyway, so what are you going to do? Y'all both messed up."

She held up a hand. "Before you go off on me, just listen. You've been trying to get Mike to talk to you and forgive you. Why? Was it because you wanted to work things out?"

"I don't know exactly. I just wanted to talk through things. The atmosphere in this house is depressing and dark. We're both unhappy. We're both stuck. We haven't done anything to move forward, whether it's together or apart. I suppose I just wanted him to acknowledge me, to see me. I wanted him to hear me."

She stood up and leaned against the kitchen island and uncorked the wine. "So, if JD hadn't died, what were you planning to do? Were you going to leave Mike for him?"

"No, I wasn't. I won't lie, I had fun with JD, and he made me feel good and sexy ... and wanted. In the beginning, I thought I was starting to fall in love with him. But when I found out I was pregnant, I realized that I didn't want to be with him, or raise a baby with him. It was stupid, but it's like the pregnancy woke me up. At the same time, I didn't know what I was going to do about Mike either. I'd thought of leaving him. I didn't know what I wanted to do then, but after all that has happened, I know what I want now."

She raised a perfectly shaped brow. "And what's that?"

"I want him to leave. I don't know where we will end up, but I know that I can't deal with sharing this house with him. I need to process all the events of the last year without our resentment for each other lurking in every corner of any room we're in together. He needs to go."

Gallery of Lies

***

When Mike walked in through the door, I still sat at the kitchen table. He leaned in the same spot Cheryl had been standing in earlier. I hadn't expected the feeling of dread that came over me. I loved him; I knew that in my heart, but my brain sent a different signal. As he looked at me, all I felt was the big knot you get in your chest when you find out someone close to you has died. Maybe I had died, and this was hell. Or, perhaps this is how it felt when a marriage was dead.

He started talking to me. I just stared at him. I wanted to attack him again. I wanted to stab him. My head throbbed. I took deep breaths in my nose and out through my mouth.

Don't cry. Don't get hysterical. Stay calm. Keep breathing.

I didn't know what he was saying, so I interrupted him.

"Mike, I want you to leave. Don't make me fight you about this. I'm not going to move out, and we can't stay in here together."

He stopped talking and looked at me, eyebrows furrowed.

"But Mona, how can you say I need to leave? I brought you home from the hospital after you cheated on me."

He had entered the kitchen looking like a pitiful child, but now he stood up straight.

"I think we need to discuss this. We can figure it out. We can't figure it out if we are separated."

"Mike, the house is in my name isn't it?"

He pulled up short. It was low for me to throw that in his face, but I wanted him to know I was serious.

"So leave. I don't want you here."

"Ok, you're right, maybe we need some time to think. I will go to a hotel for a few days."

"No Mike, not for a few days. You need to leave. Take what you can now, but you need to come and get the rest later."

"So you're putting me out after I nursed you back to health while you're pregnant with another man's child? I can't believe this shit, Mona. No matter what I did, I never fucked around on you Mona. Never..."

I felt myself jumping up out of the chair. He held his hands up. "Mona, sit down. I'm not going to let you hit me again."

I stopped but stood there panting like a rabid dog. Mike backed up.

"Fine, Mona. I will leave. Only because I don't want to get physical with you, but I don't understand how you can be this selfish."

I had no words to reply. I didn't care. My husband finally left the kitchen. I sat back down in the chair at the table. I didn't know what to do. My thoughts raced all over the place. He'd leave, and I'd be alone, but was it any different from the other dozens of times he had left me here alone to go to work or to visit his son? I kept sitting there until he walked back through the kitchen with a suitcase. He stood there and looked at me for a minute before he finally walked out the door. All the tears that I had been holding in came flooding out. I cried until I didn't have the strength to cry anymore.

CHAPTER 26

THE DOORBELL RANG. I wished my dad would just use his key. He knew how long it would take me to get up off this chair and make it to the door. I picked up my cell phone and dialed his number. He answered on the third ring.

"Dad, just use your key ok. It will take me a minute to get up there to the front."

It took about four rocks back and forth for me to gain enough forward momentum to raise myself up onto my feet. I really needed to bring one of the barstools back here to the bedroom. The recliner was comfortable but hell to get up out of.

By the time I had made it to the kitchen, he was looking in the fridge.

"Hey daddy."

He turned around with a bottle of water in his hand and his face broke into that familiar smile. He hugged me very delicately as if I would break if he squeezed too hard.

"Hey my Monie. How have you been feeling?"

I sighed. "I'm fine dad. I feel pretty good, I just get frustrated with my swollen feet and waddling everywhere."

I didn't mention that I cried in my office every morning. People kept telling me that my hormones were probably out of whack. I still hadn't found the courage to tell anyone in the office that I was separated from Mike. They knew that I'd had an accident and all, but none of them knew who JD had been to me. They thought this was Mike's baby. I didn't mention to dad that I cried myself to sleep every night either.

"Well baby that's to be expected. You are pretty far along. If I didn't know any better I would think you were about ten months."

He snickered, and I slapped him lightly on the arm.

"I know daddy, it's crazy. I have already gained forty pounds. Any more and I will have to get around with a tow truck."

I moved over to a bar stool and he helped me to situate myself on it before he sat at the kitchen table.

"I'm glad they've been letting me stay pretty immobile at work. Cheryl has been a huge help. Which reminds me, she picked up your medicine for me. It's right there on the counter."

He glanced over at the CVS package with a look of disgust on his face.

"I could have picked up my own medicine. I'm supposed to be helping you and you still trying to do everything for me like I'm not a grown man."

"I know dad, I know. I just want to make sure you get your medicine on time and don't run out."

He said, "And I know you, so I won't complain anymore ... today. You don't need to be moving around too much anyway. Do you want me to put your Christmas tree up? You usually have your decorations up by now."

Before I could stop them the tears started coming down my face. I wiped at them. My daddy jumped up faster than I had seen him move in years.

"What's wrong? Is it the baby? Are you hurting?"

"No. I don't know what's wrong with me. I'm fine... really."

He handed me a handkerchief from his pocket. He always had one. He was old school like that. Regret overtook me. Even though Mike traveled throughout the year, this was going to be the first time that we had not spent Christmas together in twelve years. He loved Christmas and he was the one that usually put all of the lights up outside the house. I didn't want to even see those lights. Everything in this stupid house that I hadn't wanted to leave reminded me of him. I was still sleeping in the guest room. I couldn't stand to look at that bed in our master bedroom. The tears started to fall again.

"Aww my Monie, tell me what's the matter. You're acting like everything is fine, but I know it can't be."

"Dad, you know we don't talk about things like that. It will be ok. I... I just need for this baby to come so that my emotions will calm down. My hormones are causing me to cry about everything."

He stood back from me. "What do you mean we don't talk about things? We talk all the time?"

"Not about the things that happened in the past."

"Mona, don't start with that again."

I sniffled. "It's true daddy. But I don't want to argue with you today."

"I know it's hard. It took me a long time to be able to get excited about anything after your mama was gone. I just sat around and drank whiskey, feeling sorry for myself. When I lost my job, it just got worse."

My eyebrows had to have been up in my hairline. "When did you lose your job? I don't remember that."

"Baby, you were young, you wouldn't remember. You know I traveled all the time. I got caught driving under the influence while I was on the road. The D.U.I went on my record and the company had to let me go. I couldn't even be mad because I knew better. It was my own fault. That's when I got the job at Sears' Home Service Center."

"I thought you stopped traveling to stay home with me."

"Naw, I wish that was the reason. It was just a bad time. My sister really helped me out with you a lot. She would have been tickled to see you waddling around like this."

I thought of Aunt Deborah's loud laugh and her smacking that damn gum all the time while she held her cigarette. She had taught me how to put on makeup. She had given me advice. I could almost hear her raspy voice. *"Mona, you can't show them boys your goodies. Keep them covered up and keep them guessing."* She had fought lung cancer with her sense of humor intact, wearing her red lipstick until the end. She had loved my mother like a sister, but I don't think she ever forgave her for the pain she caused us. I know she would've been disappointed that I followed in my mother's footsteps in the worst way. My eyes welled up again.

"Baby, it's not that I don't want to talk about things, it's just too hard to think about everything that happened and try to explain all the bad choices. It's hard to talk about all that and not go back to drinking to forget it all again... and I won't do that because I know I have to be here for you and my grandbaby. No matter what happened and no matter who left us, we've always had each other; haven't we Monie?"

I sniffed when he patted my shoulder and moved towards the door to the basement. "You're right daddy. No matter what happens we have each other."

He stood with his hand on the door, but he didn't turn back to look at me. He just said, "Now which side of the basement are those Christmas decorations on? We can at least put the wreath on the door. It will make you feel better."

I doubted it would really make me feel better, but it would make him feel better to do this for me so I let him.

CHAPTER 27

I TRIED TO GET UP off the stool and stabbing pain arced across the top of my stomach. The glass that I was holding in my hand shattered on the floor. My eyes squeezed shut and I could hear my daddy call my name. He stood in front of me then, telling me not to move while he got the broom and swept the glass and soda over to the side so that I could get off the stool. When I tried to stand up, the sharp pain shot across my stomach again and my legs gave out but dad caught me.

A fear that I had never felt before came over me. It was too early for the baby to come. Daddy had one arm around me and I could hear the fear in his voice as he talked to me.

"Mona, baby, what's wrong? I'm going to take you to the hospital."

He was leading me to the front door. I leaned on him heavily as he led me to the door and I told him to go and grab my purse out of my room. I propped myself up against the table in the foyer. While he was gone another sharp pain ripped through my body. He came back with my purse and had also thought to grab the bag that I packed from the bedroom closet. As I got in the car, a gush of wetness ran down my thighs.

Everything that happened in the hospital was a blur. The last time I was there, my baby's life had been in jeopardy, and her father died. Again I was scared to lose another life. My daddy held my hand on my left side of me while Cheryl stood on the right of me rubbing my back in small circles. Dr. Franklin came in to check on my progress or lack thereof. My cervix refused to dilate any more than four centimeters.

When the doctor came back in the next time things happened so fast. The baby's heartbeat kept slowing down with each contraction. She was in distress. Dr. Franklin called out orders for someone to prep an OR. She told me she thought it was best to go ahead and do an emergency C-section. Daddy held my hand until nurses came into prep me for the operating room. Cheryl tried to hide it, but the fear on her face increased the anxiety that had already wrapped itself around me like a vine threatening to choke me.

The next thing I knew, attendants wheeled down a long hallway with the walls and speckled ceiling tiles flying past me. I cried, terrified that one of us wouldn't make it back to the room. What if I lost this baby that I didn't even want at first? Was this all for nothing? Would I be punished in this way for my sins?

They wheeled me into the room and transferred me to a table. Nurses plugged IV tubes and beeping machines into me. Then they blocked my view of my belly with a curtain draped across my chest.

Everything below my chest was numb. The doctors and nurses talked in medical jargon that sounded so much scarier than it did on TV now that this was real. A nurse strapped my arms down. Did they think I would get up in the middle of the surgery?

At first, I didn't feel anything as the doctor worked but then suddenly there was a lot of pressure and tugging. Then I saw the tops of the medical team's covered heads as they started scrambling around. I couldn't see anything, and they didn't hold my baby up for me to see her. I needed for them to move that damn drape. I didn't hear anything. Wasn't she supposed to cry or something? I assumed the doctor was sewing me up or stapling me or whatever they did to bodies after they had been cut open.

I still couldn't hear my baby. I saw glimpses of people coming into the room and moving around frantically. Oh my God. Something was wrong. I screamed at them.

"What's wrong with my baby?"

The nurses told me everything was ok, but I didn't believe them. "Why isn't she crying?" Just as I was about to try and use superhuman strength to break my arms free, I heard the most beautiful sound in the world, the small cry at first that turned into a healthy wail.

Tears tracked down from the corner of my eyes too. Finally, a nurse held her up over the curtain for a few seconds for me to see her. It wasn't long enough for me to thoroughly examine her but she was ok. Thank God she was ok. An elation that I had never felt before filled my chest and the joy poured down my face in the form of tears. We both would be leaving this operating room alive.

***

The guest room of my house had been my master bedroom since the accident. A bassinet that my coworkers gave me at the baby shower they threw at work sat in the corner. Sunny sucked at my breast while I stared at the blanket printed with lavender butterflies draped across the arm of the rocking chair. I had looked at this arrangement for two weeks, thinking that I needed to go ahead and make this the baby's room. At some point, I needed to move back into the real master bedroom and let Sunny have this one as her own.

I didn't have any energy. I had never been so tired in my life. Yesterday afternoon she had been crying, and I didn't even hear her. Daddy happened to come over to the house and wake me up. I didn't think it was possible to sleep through all of that wailing, but I just wanted to sleep all day. I let daddy hold her. Then Cheryl came over and held her for some time. I slept some more.

I was just so exhausted. Co-workers and others had tried to warn me. I read it in articles and books on new babies. I thought I understood, but I was clueless. I didn't know it was humanly possible to be this tired. I felt like my brain was even slower, I couldn't remember anything, and I kept losing things.

Who would have thought I'd be taking care of a baby alone? It was my fault. Sometimes I didn't want to look down at her. I didn't want to see the innocent face. She would never know she was born out of anything but innocence. My hand swiped at my face. She would never know her daddy like I knew mine. JD wasn't here for this. Wherever he was, I wondered if he could see her.

Yes, I had made the decision that I didn't want to be with him before the accident, but why did he have to die? I wished he was here to look at her little nose and gray eyes. I think she had his mouth. I wiped at my face again, this time with the burp cloth. I hoped Cheryl would come by today and take the baby for a while. I was so tired. I just needed a little more sleep.

CHAPTER 28

DAD SAT IN THE CHAIR beside my bed. He held Sunny, looked down at her little face and let her grasp his finger. She had her hand wrapped around his finger, but in reality, it was he who was wrapped around hers. When he looked at that baby, the lines in his face seemed to disappear. He'd been spending every spare second he could find time with her. More time than I had, and I was in the house with her. I looked at him, and it was like the baby he was holding didn't come from my body. It felt like I was still pregnant. Why was she so calm lying in his arms? She lay there cooing and adorable as you see on the diaper commercials with the perfect babies. Whenever I held her, she squirmed and wailed until her little face was as red as an apple.

I'm certain the baby's problem with me existed because I couldn't feed her the way nature intended. Everyone told me that during breast feeding was when the bonding happened. All the books I read screamed at me that I needed to breastfeed my baby because the mother's milk was the healthiest for her. Tell my body that. If it was supposed to work that way then why couldn't I produce enough milk to keep her from starving? Every time I held her, she cried, and I cried. She hated me already. How could a baby that small already know that her mother was a failure? She already knew I was worthless, and that she was born into a broken home because I cheated on my husband.

I watched her smiling and kicking and making baby faces at my daddy. I wished he would get up and take her out of here. I didn't need him reminding me how much of a loser I was. I closed my eyes. Maybe I could go to sleep.

Daddy said, "Mona it's a beautiful day outside, why don't we take the baby out so she can see where her name came from?"

I said, "You can go ahead and take her out if you want to."

I didn't even open my eyes.

He cleared his throat. "I think it would be good for you to get out too. It's been almost two months since the C-section. I think it will be ok if you get up and start moving around some. Plus I know you want to start dropping that baby weight."

He laughed a small laugh.

"So what you trying to tell me is that I need to get my fat ass up out of this bed because I'm neglecting my baby?"

My eyes opened wide then so that I could look at him with his eyebrows knit together like he didn't know what I was talking about. He stood up and kept bouncing Sunny. Just the sound of my voice irritated her.

"Now Mona you know I didn't say that. This attitude of yours is getting out of hand. I was trying to say that maybe you want to take Sunny out for some fresh air and you may want to get some too. I was making a joke about the baby weight since you talked so much about it while you were pregnant."

Tears started running down my face. My body shook, and all I could do was wipe my eyes on the corner of my shirt. I wore a yellow maternity t-shirt decorated with poop stains and baby puke. I should be ashamed of myself. I tried to stop the tears but I couldn't. Daddy came over and started to rub my back, but the touch of his hand made me feel worse. Sunny then started wailing, and daddy stopped paying attention to me to try to get her to calm down.

He spoke baby gibberish to her and tried to put the pacifier in her mouth. She wasn't having it.

"Just take her out of here..." I sobbed. I upset my baby when I should have been caring for her. He didn't say anything else to me. He shook his head at me before he hiked Sunny up on his shoulder and carried her from the room.

***

I rolled over in the bed and saw that it had gotten dark. The scent of cooking food hung in the air. It smelled like chicken. My stomach growled. When was the last time I ate? I heard cabinets opening and dishes clinking. A few minutes later, daddy stood in the doorway to my room holding a tray of food. I don't know where he'd found that tray. Mike had served me breakfast in bed on that tray when we were newlyweds. Tears sprang to my eyes.

"Mona are you awake?" he whispered.

I pushed myself up on my elbows and scooted back in the bed until my back was against the headboard, and reached over to turn on the lamp. I glanced over and saw Sunny sleeping in the bassinet.

"Yeah, I'm up."

My voice sounded like it was rusted. I reached up and felt my eyelids and the rest of my face. I was sure it was swollen and puffy. My eyes felt as if they weren't all the way opened. Maybe I should turn the light back off. Daddy came and put the tray down on the bed. He had cooked baked chicken, yellow rice, and green beans. He hadn't made a meal for me in years, probably since I moved into my own place after college. I was starving.

He left the room then came back with a plate of his own and sat down in the chair that he sat in earlier holding Sunny. We ate in silence, but I could tell that he wanted to say something. When I was a teenager, he would always cook me something I liked when he had bad news for me.

Daddy looked at me now, the serene look he'd had on his face long gone. "Mona, baby, it's going to be ok. I've been hoping you would bounce back, but you're not. I think you might need to talk to somebody. You might be depressed."

I smacked my lips. "Of course I'm depressed. My life is a wreck right now. People say things get better with time. I wish time would hurry up and pass by."

"Naw Monie, I think it's a little more serious than that. I've been reading about women after they have babies who get that baby blues. But I think you are worse off than that. I talked with Ms. Thornton at church... ."

"Wait, you were talking to who? Since when have you two talked?"

"Look, girl, don't try to change the subject. I talked to her on the phone. She called me and asked how you were doing since you haven't been back up to volunteer at the nursing home in so long."

"Oh, so you're buddies now? All this time I have been trying to get you to call her... "

He cut me off. "Exactly, I didn't call her; she called me to ask me to volunteer for something. But while I was on the phone, I happened to mention how you had been acting and she said for me to look up some things on the computer."

"And you actually turned on your computer and looked at something?"

"Well no I didn't. But I looked up some stuff on my phone. Cheryl had to help me with that Google app though. I had to install things on there to make it work."

At that statement, I think my mouth hung open. It had taken me months to get him to switch over from that flip phone that he'd been holding on to since the first Bush was president. Then when I got him to use it, he had refused to use any features besides the phone. He still won't respond to my text messages. Instead, he calls me every time I text him.

I felt myself getting angry. "Well at any rate dad, I don't know why all of you think it's appropriate to go and psychoanalyze me on the internet. I read plenty about that before I had Sunny. And I am not suffering from postpartum depression. I'm just a little sad. I am not thinking about killing myself or my baby. So can we stop this nonsense please?"

He sat there quiet for a minute, and so did I.

"Well, I'm just trying to help baby girl. I hate to see you like this. You hardly want to play with your baby or spend time with her, and you are her mama. These first few weeks is time for y'all to bond..."

"I'm so sick of hearing that. We aren't bonding. I can't breastfeed her. All she does is cry. She doesn't respond that way when you hold her. I'm trying. I'm scared to mess this up -- to mess her up. She won't have a father in her life. All she'll have is me, and what if I'm not good enough? I've messed up everything."

"Mona," he said. "As a parent, you will always be scared. We all hope that we are doing the right things for our children. We all wonder if we are screwing our kids up. It's natural to be scared. You've been reading those books, but there is no instruction manual. You can only do the best you can and stop pitying yourself. You have to do it for Sunny."

The next day, Dad didn't come by the house. In some ways, I was glad he didn't come over because I didn't want him in my face telling me what I needed to do. Then the reality sank in that I had to do everything for Sunny. He usually spent a few hours here every day, giving me a break from her non-stop wailing. When she woke up, it felt like she knew her grandfather wouldn't be around. She saw me and screamed at the top of her lungs. My head hurt. I got up and put her formula in bottles and sat back down to feed her. I tried rocking her in the chair, but she didn't like that. I put her in the baby bouncer, and that kept for entertained for about five minutes before she started crying again. I held her and paced up and down the hallway. When I walked past the full-length mirror on the back of the closet, I felt ashamed.

When was the last time I had combed my hair? If I weren't careful, it would dread up, and I would have to cut it off to get it untangled. I hadn't taken a shower yesterday. Had I bathed the day before that? It didn't matter, because the baby never gave me a chance to do anything for myself. She barely gave me time to breathe. Without dad, I didn't get to eat or to nap like I had done every day since bringing her home.

I walked into the other room and left the baby crying in the bassinet. I could still hear her. I didn't know what to do. I was going to lose it soon. How could my dad act this hateful by not coming over here today? How was I supposed to handle this without help? I went in the bathroom, turned the shower on full blast, and closed the door. I didn't get in; I just sat on the toilet sobbing. I knew I shouldn't leave her alone like this, but I just needed a break for a few minutes where I couldn't hear her crying.

After about five minutes of hiding out in the bathroom, I felt so guilty, I stood up and opened the door. I didn't hear anything.

I ran back in the bedroom and looked at her. I picked her up, and she startled awake. Oh my God, I thought she'd stopped breathing or something. She started to cry again, but I didn't walk away from her anymore. Maybe my dad was right. I needed help. I had left my baby alone. I was stupid and careless. I sat with the baby in the rocking chair and fed her again. She finally fell back asleep. I suppose she had tired her little self out crying. I pulled out my phone and looked up therapists for women with postpartum depression. I'd never heard of it before, but I found one that offered online counseling and set up an appointment.

I set up twice weekly sessions with Dr. Martin, and we met through video conferencing. I often was able to sit there with Sunny in my arms during the counseling sessions. Eventually, she became calmer with me. I learned that when I was upset, she could feel my emotions and cried too. It was in those therapy sessions that I started to bond with my baby.

CHAPTER 29

CARS SLOWED DOWN as they passed me, people craned their necks and pointed. I looked down at my leg, and blood ran down to my ankle. Glass and debris scattered across the pavement. The motorcycle lay twisted off to the side of the grass. I had to get help. Could someone stop to help me? I think we had an accident. Where was JD? I limped down the pavement, over onto the shoulder. A few feet ahead I saw the back of his leather jacket. It was JD there on the asphalt but his legs twisted at an unnatural angle. I limped over to him as fast as I could drag my leg. I struggled to turn him over. Was he breathing? I lifted the visor covering his face. Mike's face lay under the visor; his brown dead eyes stared at me. I screamed...

I startled myself awake from the nightmare. Sunny lay in the bed next to me. She stirred and whined but didn't wake up. I got up and placed her and a bottle in her baby carrier and headed upstairs to my studio. I hadn't touched a paintbrush since Mike had brought me home from the hospital. Dr. Martin had tried for weeks to encourage me to get back to painting, but I knew it would bring up to many still raw emotions. But that night, it called out to me. I needed to do something with all of this restlessness. I felt driven to do something with my hands, to find some way to open up my brain and pour out all of these thoughts.

Sunny slept soundly for a change, but unfortunately, her mama did not. In the first couple of months after the accident, I didn't remember anything that had happened, but it had been coming back to me through my nightmares in bits and pieces.

I put Sunny's carrier down on the floor next to my easel and queued up some old school music, soulful with its sultry vocals and deep bass beats. One of my favorite songs came on. Rose Royce told me how love don't live here anymore. I dipped brushes in paints and splashed them up onto the canvas. I didn't know what I was painting until the images started to take form. The black and midnight blue background gave way to slashes of red. The music must have been soothing to Sunny because she barely stirred as I moved the brush furiously over the surface of the canvas.

Finally, exhausted, I put the brush down and stood back. It was the scene from my dream. A mangled motorcycle. Two figures twisted on the pavement. Police lights. Brake lights. The beginning of the ending of my life as I knew it. I sat on the floor, and the tears rolled from my eyes. My stomach hurt. My chest hurt. I lay there on the rough floor. I didn't deserve to feel any comfort. I pillowed my head on my folded arms gulping and gasping for air.

I didn't remember falling asleep, but Sunny's high pitched cry woke me up. She had to be hungry. I had no clue what time it was. I sat up and felt the tug of a crook in my neck. I had been stupid to lie on the floor like that. I picked her up and put her bottle to her mouth. I looked up at my creation. Why in the world would I have painted such a horrible thing? Luckily, no one would ever see this. When Sunny finished feeding, I put her back into her carrier and took the painting off the easel. I lay it up against the wall in the corner and put an old gray tarp over it. No one needed to see this, including me. I never wanted to think about that moment ever again. One of these days I would come back up here and dispose of it, but for now, Sunny and I went back downstairs to my room. The clock read 4:17 A.M. and when I finally did get back in the bed, I didn't have any other dreams for the rest of that night.

***

For the next few weeks, I found myself up in the studio a lot of nights painting while Sunny snuggled down in her carrier. Sometimes she whined, and I kept her strapped in the soft carrier against my chest while I painted. I think I had found my secret weapon. The music on the jazz station kept her soothed and quiet.

A few times daddy had come over to find Sunny and I asleep on the floor of the studio. A few days later he came over with a big box from Wal-Mart that held a futon. I couldn't do anything but laugh.

He scolded me as he removed the packing from the box. "If you're gonna have my grandbaby up there in that studio, the least you could do is have something comfortable up there to lay down on."

I let him put the seat together and ended up being grateful for his interference. The next week, a playpen appeared up there when Sunny and I came home from the pediatrician. I don't know why he thought Sunny needed it up there; she wasn't even crawling yet.

"Just wait," he said. "She'll be crawling before you know it."

And before I knew it, she crawled around that playpen as fast as her little juicy legs would take her while I painted.

CHAPTER 30

I SAT IN THE KITCHEN at the table and watched Sunny crawl around her little play pen exploring every Inch of the padded floor beneath her. She could eagle eye any speck of foreign matter no matter how minuscule and put in her mouth. Just seeing her curiosity amazed me to no end.

The phone rang, and I looked down at it, surprised at the name on the screen.

"Hello."

"Hello, is this Mona?"

"Yes, it is. Is this Val?"

"Yeah, child, it's me. How have you been doing? You were on my mind this morning."

I laughed, "I was? That's funny, what made you think about me?"

"Well, I don't know. I just had you on my heart. I haven't seen you since Tasha's birthday party. How are you?"

I gave the standard response. "I've been doing fine. Speaking of Tasha, how is she?"

"Child, she is doing just fine. As a matter of fact, she just got engaged to old dry as a piece of toast, Steve."

I couldn't help but laugh. "Oh yeah, well that's great. Congratulations."

Then I remembered our very first conversation in art class and her trying to hook Tasha up with JD. A pang of sadness that I hadn't felt in weeks washed over me. JD's face flashed in my mind. She said something else that I had missed in my reverie.

"You still there?"

I cleared my throat before answering. "Yes Val, I'm here. I'm sorry though I didn't hear what you said."

"I said, how have you really been?"

"I told you I've been fine. Work has been good. I've been painting."

Val's voice had changed to a more serious tone. "Oh have you? That's good. Painting can be very therapeutic. I don't paint a whole lot, but I do turn to my sewing sometimes when I need comfort."

I didn't understand her comments. Was she implying that I was troubled? She wouldn't know that.

Val continued to chatter. "Why don't we meet up for some coffee or desert one weekend?"

She caught me off guard.

"Umm... well, I think that would be nice. We should do that sometime."

"How about this Saturday about two?"

"Umm, I won't be able to get out on Saturday I don't think. I won't have anyone to keep my... I won't be able to make it."

Why hadn't I mentioned Sunny?

"Well if it would be better for you I can come to your house. I would love to see what you have been painting."

She was being pushy, or nosy. I thought nosy was more like it. "Ok. I, ummm, sure you can come over here. I mean it's not much to look at, just a bunch of stuff. None of its all that special."

She laughed, and it reminded me of wind chimes. "I'm sure it will be good. I want to visit with you. So will Saturday at two work? I'll bring some treats so don't worry about anything."

"Oh, ok Val, that's fine..."

"Child I gotta go. I was cooking dinner and think I may have left the chicken in the oven too long. See you on Saturday. Text me your address."

Before I could say another word, she hung up the phone. Now I knew how Tasha felt. I wondered if she was bringing her, she hadn't said. How was I going to explain why I hadn't mentioned that I'd had a baby since the last time she had seen me. What kind of mother doesn't gush on and on about their baby? I looked over at Sunny, making happy noises and chewing on her toy. That beautiful little girl was nothing to be ashamed of.

***

Saturday emerged bright and warm. I got out of bed and made some breakfast for myself after I fed Sunny. I put the dishes in the dishwasher and made sure the bathrooms were clean. I tidied up the den fluffing the cushions on the sofa. At that moment was when I realized I felt downright nervous about Val's visit today. Guilt flowed up into my chest as I thought about how I had not mentioned my baby. I didn't want to feel ashamed, but I was. I didn't want her to judge me, to see that I had done terrible things to my marriage and betrayed my husband. I didn't want to be one of those women that everyone talked about with pity. The world was full of hypocrites. Men cheated all the time and received a pass because we think, "That's how men are. They are all dogs." It's expected.

If I'd heard a story about a woman like me three years ago, I would have been one of those severe judges. Holding myself in such high regard, saying that I would never break up my marriage over something so stupid. I'd always said things like, if it were me I would leave Mike. Why cheat? Now I knew how hard it was to stay happily married, even when you thought you'd found the soul mate that people talked about. I had that life once. But I didn't have it anymore.

I filled the bowl on the kitchen table with lemons as I had seen in the magazines. The kitchen island shone in the sunlight streaming through the windows as I Windexed the hell out of it. Sunny cooed and giggled from her spot on the floor. She was pulling up on one of the chairs testing her little juicy brown legs. She will be an early walker I thought. My dad had always told me that I started walking when I was ten months old. She was probably going to be like her mama.

After we had waged war on every speck of dust downstairs, I hitched Sunny up on to my hip and headed up to the studio. I put her down into the playpen and started to clean up all of the spilled paint. I cleaned brushes that I had left in the sink at the last session. I took the canvases out of the closet and spread them out on different surfaces around the room, so they were easier to view. The most recent painting I'd worked on was from a snapshot of Sunny's hand in my dad's big brown wrinkled hand. I carefully leaned it against the counter in the middle of the other paintings. The others may not be that great, but I was particularly proud of that one.

The last canvas I pulled out sat covered in a sheet facing the wall in the back corner of the room. It was the painting that I had done of the accident. I hadn't looked at it since I put it in the back of the closet. It looked like a mess of paint and bad memories jumbled up on the dark background. I put it back in the corner with the sheet over it. I wouldn't display a painting for Val that depicted the beginning of the end of my old way of life.

By the time I finished tidying up and bathed both myself and Sunny, the doorbell rang. I pasted a smile on my face and answered the door to Val's wide smile that sparkled in her eyes. She held a pink box in one hand and immediately wrapped the other arm around me in a warm hug that I had not understood how much I needed until then.

I stepped back so that she could come in.

"Oh Mona, this is a beautiful home you have here."

I said "thank you" as she swiveled her head around, looking up at the ceiling and around the foyer.

She held up the box. "I told you I would bring treats. My friend owns a bakery, and she makes the finest pastries in Atlanta. I didn't know what you liked so I told her to give me one of everything. I hope you ain't on no diet."

She laughed her wind chime laugh, and it made me feel lighter.

"Diet you say? I don't even know what that word means." We both giggled.

At that moment we turned as Sunny came rolling into the foyer in her walker babbling. Evidently, my daughter had to tell me that I was taking too long at the door. Val smiled down at her, handed me the box and reached for my baby.

"Oh my goodness now who's this adorable little angel?"

"That's my baby girl, Sunny."

She gave me a sidelong look as she picked the chubby little girl up. Sunny went right to her like she had met this woman when she hadn't seen her a day in her seven months.

"Now why didn't you tell me you had had a baby when I was talking to you?"

I looked away, "Oh I thought I mentioned it."

She pursed her lips at me. "Child you know you didn't mention this baby."

Sunny had her fat hands on Val's cheeks like she was playing pat-a-cake. Val couldn't contain her laughter.

"She is such a happy baby, what is her name."

"Her name is Sunny."

Val bent over with laughter then. "That fits her just right. This child has a happy spirit on her."

She held Sunny while she played with Val's dreadlocks.

I warned her. "She will tug them Val so you might not want to let her do that."

"I don't mind, child. It's been a long time since I held a baby. I'm waiting on my daughter to go ahead and make me some grandchildren."

I put the pastries on the table and offered Val a seat while I started the coffee maker and got paper plates and napkins from under the counter. I opened the box and selected what looked like a chocolate croissant from the array of beautifully done pastries that made my mouth water.

"I also have tea if you prefer."

"No baby, I'm a coffee drinker even though I have had to limit myself to half a cup a day per my doctor's orders."

Val pulled what looked like a cream cheese Danish out of the box. We sat there and made small talk as we finished up our pastries. Sunny nibbled on a piece of blueberry muffin with the two teeth that poked through her little gums before Val finally said she was ready to see the paintings.

***

When we walked up the stairs and entered the studio, I put Sunny in her playpen with her rattle toy and let Val roam around the room.

"This is a wonderful studio space. You have the best light up here."

She wandered around, looking at the shelves and the storage space first. I hadn't expected her to make full exploration of everything in the room. I was glad that I had straightened everything up in there. She then went over to the side of the room where I had all of my paintings on display. She looked at the still life paintings that I had done of flowers and fruit before I had taken any art classes at all. There was a painting of Sunny crawling on the grass, a close up of her chubby face. I had painted my dad's profile as he looked down at his only grandchild. There was a hazy abstract form of my mother from my memories as a child. When Val meandered over to the first painting that I had done in the class, she made a noise of recognition.

"Now I recognize this from the first week of our painting class. I thought you were a good painter when we first started, but looking at how you have improved your skills and expressiveness, I'm impressed. I don't know if I ever mentioned this, but my first cousin owns an art gallery in Castleberry Hills."

My eyebrows shot up. "I have been to that gallery. They feature a lot of new African American artists right?"

She turned to me and smiled. "Yes, they do. My cousin's name is Phillip Gaines, and he's always looking for new talent to feature. Have you ever thought about doing a gallery show?"

I laugh escaped my mouth. "No, of course not. I'm not an artist. I paint as a hobby and a stress reliever of sorts."

As we talked, she continued to walk around the room and eventually got to the paintings in the back with the sheet thrown over them.

"Oh my, what are these?"

"Wait, Val! Those aren't... "

Before I could say another word, she had lifted the corner of the sheet revealing the scene of the accident that changed my life.

I ran over and snatched the sheet out of her hand.

"I don't want anyone to look at those Val. I'm sorry."

She took a step back from me, a hand up to her chest.

"I'm sorry, I didn't realize you didn't want me to see those. I'm so sorry."

I felt my eyes water and turned my back to her.

"I don't mean to seem crazy, but those are too personal."

Val just put a hand on my shoulder. "Baby it's ok. The one thing about our art is that most of the time it shows the deepest and most vulnerable part of us. That's why singers put out the best albums when they are going through hard times in their personal lives."

"You're right, but I don't want people to judge me. What these paintings represent… I can never forgive myself. I took betrayal to a whole other level. I can never forgive myself for what I did."

I looked over at Sunny, still playing and ignoring us.

"When you are ready, you will show me. I'm not pushing you. I know that you have things that you don't want to show me. I know you have some demons. But sometimes our shame is increased because we try to keep things in the dark, scared every time somebody so much as lights a match. You take control when you put it in the light, it no longer has power over you anymore."

Sunny cooed, and I reached for my baby. She put her arms around my neck like she knew I needed her comfort. I squeezed her, and she talked her baby language.

"Mamamamamama," Sunny cooed.

I held the sheet in my left hand. I tugged at it while I held my daughter and the covering fell away from the stacked canvases. I didn't try to stop the tears from streaming down my face. Val approached the stack slowly and looked at the painting on top that depicted the scene of the accident. She didn't say anything to me; she just studied the canvas before moving it to the side to reveal the image of JD in silhouette against the sunset on his motorcycle. The blue bike obviously his even though the helmet covered his face. The next canvas was of him with his back to the viewer, spreading paint onto his canvas. The next one a close up of his face, so close there was only one eye, his nose and part of his lips in the painting. I had painted that one after a dream where we made love. He had been on top of me looking down into my face. The next one was of my husband with steely anger in his eyes, his freckles defined. Looking at that one made me turn away.

"Mona, these paintings are extraordinary. I can feel your soul and your pain. They tell a story. I don't know the whole story, but I suspect that I can piece it together. But this is beautiful. I know it's painful. I look at this painting of JD, and all I can remember is sitting at his funeral, knowing why his casket remained closed. I looked for you there but didn't think much about it when you weren't. I saw the chemistry that had developed between the two of you by the end of the class sessions. It has to hurt you to show me this, but it takes courage. I can tell that you've been hiding. That you didn't tell me about that beautiful baby tells me a lot about what you're feeling. She's not anything to be ashamed of. She is a blessing no matter what. She represents life and what you should be doing, living."

The tears wet my face, but they had stopped running down my cheeks. I cleared my throat.

"But there's so much. If I told you everything, I don't know that you would still say what you are saying. It has been tough."

Val just smiled at me.

"We all have things in our past that we aren't so proud of. One thing I'm going to do though, is I'm going to tell my cousin about you. I think you need to be showing this art. You are an artist even if you don't claim it."

After I dried my face, I walked Val back downstairs. She gave me a long hug before she kissed Sunny on the cheek and walked out the front door. I felt lighter than I had in a long time as I put Sunny down to bed that night. Val had been right; maybe it was time that I lit that match myself.

CHAPTER 31

THE STAFF MEETING was coming up in thirty minutes, and I sat at my computer getting some last minute notes together. I took a big gulp of coffee and then stifled a yawn. Sunny had not been cooperative last night waking at two am ready to play with mommy. I wondered if I had time to run to the corner to get a five-hour energy drink. My cell phone vibrated on my desk with a number that I didn't recognize on the screen. I answered quickly hoping it wasn't someone from the daycare.

"Hello, may I speak to Mrs. Jacobs?"

"Speaking..."

"Good morning ma'am, this is Phillip Gaines. My cousin Valerie gave me your number. I'm the owner of Greenwich art gallery on Marietta St. She told me that I needed to get a look at your art and talk with you about doing business together."

"Wow... Oh my gosh. I can't believe Val did that. She mentioned something to me about doing a show, but I didn't think she was serious. I haven't prepared for this call."

He laughed in a raspy tone. "It's no problem. I know how my cousin operates. When would be a better time to call you and discuss some things, maybe set up a meeting so that I can see what you have?"

"Well, this is not the best time, I have a meeting in a few minutes, it's better to reach me after seven if that's possible."

"That's great; I will give you a call then if that's ok with you. I look forward to talking to you this evening. You have a good day."

"You too."

I ended the call. Wow, I had no idea what to do next. My watch told me that I had five minutes to get to the conference room. I decided that I would take my laptop to the meeting with me. It would be a good time to look at information about art galleries.

***

When Mr. Gaines called me back that night, we made an appointment for me to show him my art. I discovered that artists usually had professional photographs of their art to send to gallery owners. I didn't have that. I also had no idea of how the business worked. I stayed on the computer researching the subject until one in the morning. Later that night, Sunny had decided she would sleep peacefully. Instead of taking advantage of the quiet baby to sleep, I sat up wide awake. I couldn't pull myself away from the computer nervous about the possibilities.

When I got home from work the next day, I dug out my camera and decided that I would attempt to take presentable photos of my art. I went into my studio while the light was still good and took pictures at the best angles that I could muster. Then I created an online photo gallery and sent Mr. Gaines the link. I had set up a time for him to come to look at my art on Saturday.

I called Cheryl to see if she would watch Sunny. I didn't think I needed to have her crawling around for this meeting.

"Hey, Cheryl."

"What's going on girl?"

"Can you watch Sunny on Saturday? I have something that I need to do around noon."

"Sure, you know that's my favorite munchkin. What's going on?"

I didn't want to say anything yet because who knew if this would happen, but Cheryl and I had come a long way since the accident, and I didn't want to keep anything from her.

"Well, I don't know if anything will come out of it, but you know all of those paintings I have up in my studio?"

"Yeah..."

"This woman, Val, who I took the art class with has a cousin that owns an art gallery. He's coming over to consider my art for a showing."

A sound that I could only describe as a piglet like squeal came through the line.

"That's great Mona! I always told you that you had a real talent for painting. I mean, haven't you always talked about doing something creative and getting out of banking. This could be the start of a new career."

"Whoa Cheryl, I don't want to get ahead of myself. I created that stuff in my lowest darkest days. Who knows if I could be a real artist? Hell, I hope I never have any more of that type of artistic inspiration in my life ever again. I know drama makes for good art, but I am over drama."

"Who determines what makes you a real artist? If you paint, aren't you an artist? If you get a show that makes you a real artist boo. I'm so excited for you."

This sentiment was why I loved my friend. I forgot how supportive she could be, something I would never take for granted again.

I laughed, "You are right I guess. We will see what Mr. Gaines says."

"Girl, now you have a connection, if he doesn't see that it's good, then you will simply have to put your stuff out there until you find someone that does. But forget all that. He's going to love it, and he's going to see nothing but dollar signs for all the money you could make his little gallery."

We both laughed and then talked a few more minutes before we got off the phone.

She had hyped me up. I hoped I didn't get disappointed. An art show could be the breakthrough that I needed.

***

Mr. Gaines turned out to be a short brown skinned man with a handsome face and kind eyes. He wore his graying hair cut short and lined up neat. He was impeccably dressed in a gray suit when he stopped by to look at my art. He cracked an easy smile that let me see the family resemblance between him and Val. I liked him instantly, and he let me know that he loved my art. By the time he left, it looked as if we would be doing business together.

Pinterest became my best friend. I found a wealth of information about getting ready for an art exhibition. I never knew how much work went into making an art show happen beyond supplying the art. I set up time with Mr. Gaines to visit the space. With camera and sketchbook in hand, I meandered through the gallery taking pictures of the room to determine which of my paintings would go where. Sherry, the curator of the gallery, walked with me and gave me advice on which pieces she thought should go where. She also gave me some names of framers, but I decided that I would hang the art unframed. That decision would save me a few coins.

At work, I had things to do, but I couldn't help myself. This upcoming show was the first time I'd been excited about anything in months, so I threw myself into all aspects of the exhibition. Mr. Gaines had told me that it would be a good idea to have a website because buyers expected artists to have a web presence. I used my lunch break at work (give or take a few hours) to set up my website. I used the pictures I'd taken of my art and put a bio out there. When it came to my artist's statement, a statement of my purpose, I didn't know what to write. I looked at some other artists' sites, and all of them had some grand reason for creating art and lists of inspirations and art histories that they had studied. I didn't want to write that my art was the result of a broken marriage. I didn't put anything there for now and published the site.

I tried not to let my hopes get too high about the success of this show, but I couldn't help but imagine myself a full-time artist. Fantasizing about leaving my job at the bank became effortless after Jimmy's gossiping ass came into my office to tell me that word on the grapevine was that Ben was at the top of the list for promotion to regional accounting manager. I held the position of branch accounting manager for far longer and had way more experience than Ben, but he had probably trashed me while I was out of work so that he could sell himself to management for the position. It pissed me off, but then again my perspective had changed since the accident. I didn't think I wanted the additional work and hours required for the position now that I had my daughter and she only had me.

Before the end of the month, I had business and postcards ordered and on the way. I drug Cheryl with me to boutique after boutique trying to find the perfect dress to wear along with shoes with heels high enough to be classy and low enough to be comfortable. Mr. Gaines finalized the design of the show, and I approved the layout. Then, finally, it was opening night.

CHAPTER 32

I DECIDED TO WEAR a black Gucci dress to the opening. It had a white ruffled collar at the neck and hugged my hips. The baby weight was pretty much gone. My three-inch heels were conservative since I would be walking around all night talking to prospective buyers. I yanked at my hair. Should I have gone for straight instead of my natural curls? I wanted people to notice the art and not me. Were the pearls I wore too much? When I drove up to the back parking lot of the gallery, Mr. Gaines met me at the back door.

"We will be opening in about thirty minutes. The servers are ready with the hors d'oeuvres and the wine. I think it's going to be a good showing."

I tugged at my dress. "I'm nervous. It's like baring my soul to so many people that don't even know the real story behind this art. They'll probably figure some things out. I'm second guessing putting my personal life out there on display."

Mr. Gaines rested his big hand on my shoulder. "Mona, the only one that truly knows what those paintings are about is you. People will guess at the meaning, but people buy art based on how they like it, and how it speaks to their personal experiences. In the end, they don't care what it meant to the artist. Some people buy art because it matches their new couch. Don't worry. When you talk to them, you don't have to tell the whole story. Just be personable. People buy more when they like the artist."

He led me out to the gallery. My breath hitched to see all of the paintings hung and everything set up. The white walls were the perfect backdrop for the canvases with the showcase lighting shining down on them. Small high top tables were scattered throughout the room on the red painted concrete floor.

Fresh flowers rested in vases through the corners of the room. The atmosphere felt elegant, and the vibrant colors of my paintings popped perfectly in the space with its wall of glass facing the traffic on the street. People driving by would get a good glimpse of the paintings, hopefully, enough of a view for them to venture into the gallery to see more. The wait staff wore all black and lingered in the back waiting for the doors to open so they could start their service.

I walked through the space, eager to go through the gallery as if I was one of the people that would see the show for the first time tonight. At the front of the gallery hung the paintings that I had created of my father holding Sunny and the one that I painted of Cheryl laughing with her eyes crinkled shut like she did when something was stomach-achingly funny. She would get a kick out of that one since she had never seen it before. I walked towards the back, passing by the paintings of Sunny, Mike, and JD. I reached the back, where showcased by itself, was the painting of the accident that I'd titled "Revelation." The extra-large canvas seemed to blaze in the space. I had to quell the urge to rip one of the tablecloths from the table and throw it over the image. God, I hoped I was ready for this.

The doors for the show opened at 6:45 p.m. Mr. Gaines advice came to the forefront of my mind as people started to trickle in. Moving around the space, I gave people time to walk around and grab food and drink before I began to introduce myself and talk about the art. Sipping slowly on my champagne so that I didn't get too tipsy, I answered questions about the art. Mr. Gaines was right about one thing, people didn't ask probing questions. One woman asked me about my inspiration while another one asked me what story my art was telling. I told them that my paintings portrayed a rough time in my life surrounding a tragic accident and the birth of my daughter. I said this in several different ways, and this seemed to be enough of an explanation. The other questions were more about my studio space, and how I had become an artist. I relaxed and exhaled. I was even starting to enjoy myself. I felt even better when Cheryl and my dad arrived.

Dad had dressed up in his sharpest blue suit. I'd told him that a suit wasn't necessary. He'd replied that he hadn't been to anything this fancy before other than a few weddings, so he wanted to dress the part. Beside him, Cheryl wore a cobalt blue sweater dress that made me wonder where I could get one. My dad smiled broadly, it took ten years off his face.

"Monie!" He exclaimed. "Wow, this is just beautiful." He turned around in a circle with his arms out. "You know I never been to anything this fancy. I didn't even know black folks were this interested in art. I'm so proud of you for doing this."

My eyes welled up at his pride. Cheryl hugged me also.

"Girl this is remarkably nice. I mean, this is extra bougie too. I've been to art galleries before, but I have never been friends of the artist. This event feels upscale, and it's extremely well put together. I'm impressed... thoroughly." She gave me a high five. "You did that, girl."

Val showed up all smiles. The older woman looked stunning in a maroon dress that stopped right below the knee. The dress swirled around her legs and showed that her petite figure was still shapely. I introduced her to Cheryl, and Val said hello to dad. I noticed that he seemed to be standing a little straighter. He smiled at Val and complimented her dress. She giggled. The sound had me raising an eyebrow in Cheryl's direction. She smiled back at me and shrugged. I think they were flirting with each other, and I didn't know how to handle that at the moment. So I excused myself, and I told them to look around while I continued to talk to people.

A few minutes later I heard a loud squeal that told me that Cheryl had seen her likeness in the back. I heard people laughing along with applause, and when I turned the corner, she posed by the painting as my dad snapped a picture with his phone. I would let them get away with that particular bit of photography even though it wasn't allowed in the gallery. Knowing that this was my show felt terrific. I couldn't believe it was such a success. We'd invited a few people from the local press to cover the show, and I gave some short interviews.

It was almost ten o'clock, and the exhibition wound down to a close. My cheeks ached from smiling and talking, and I couldn't wait to get out of my heels. I had gone to powder my nose, thinking about the number of sales we'd made. I walked out of the ladies room and headed to a group of people that I had not greeted earlier. When I got near the painting of Sunny a lone figure stood there studying the painting. Though he stood with his back to me, I would always recognize his form in a crowd. I stopped dead in my tracks when he turned around. Here was the last person that I had ever expected to see here tonight-- Mike.

He looked at me like he was just as surprised to see me even though this was my show.

He said, "Mona."

"What are you doing here?" I said.

He looked around then back at me. Evidently, he didn't know what to say, but I recognized the look of anger on his face.

"I came here to congratulate you on the exhibition," he said.

"Thanks... thank you... how did you know?"

He cut me off, "I came here with the intention to wish you success on the show but when I walked around the corner and saw my face up there and then that other dude's picture on the other side... Well, I don't know what the hell to say now, Mona."

My head snapped back.

"Look Mike. This isn't the time or place for a confrontation. Who invited you anyway?"

He looked towards Cheryl, and I should have known that she had been keeping in contact with him. She was a traitor just like my dad for talking to him, but I wasn't surprised.

"I hear things."

His eyes traveled over me from head to toe.

"I always knew you liked to paint, but I didn't know you could do all this. These images are so much more than I expected. It's too much."

He looked over at the image of JD hanging across from where he stood. His eyes looked sad, and I know that my expression must have matched his.

"I never would have invited you to this Mike. This isn't... I'm trying to say, this show wasn't meant to hurt you."

"How could you think this wouldn't hurt? I thought I wanted to see this, but I didn't expect to see some of these images. Didn't you need my permission to display this?" His hand swept in the general direction of his image on the wall.

"Well Mike, no I did not. This is an artistic work. You were a part of what I was going through when I painted these works. I was going to leave this piece out of the show, but the gallery owner insisted I show it."

Gallery of Lies

He turned his back on me then as my father walked towards us with Cheryl trailing him.

Dad's low voice rumbled with seriousness, "Mike, let's take a walk."

Dad took hold of Mike's arm and led him back toward the exit. I expected Mike to try and make a scene, but I guess he thought better of it. My dad's body language told him he didn't want any problems. I'm glad he didn't try it, my dad would have probably tried to whoop his ass. I didn't need both of them getting arrested. Through the glass, I could see Mike walk away down the street without incident.

I refused to cry in here. I looked around to see who had noticed the confrontation. I saw a couple of eyes on us, but I think most people hadn't noticed. I prayed they hadn't anyway.

I felt a hand on my back and turned to look into Cheryl's face.

"Did you invite him here?"

She put a hand on my arm. "No Mona, I didn't invite him, but he's been keeping tabs on you. I might have mentioned that you had been painting, but I think Ray told him you had an exhibit coming up. I don't think he gave him details, so he must have looked it up and found the date."

"My dad already let it slip that he's been talking to him. I don't like that he saw all of this. I don't know what I was thinking. I let Mr. Gaines talk me into displaying that painting. I should've known better."

I walked away from Cheryl and grabbed another glass of champagne from one of the trays. I pasted a smile on my face and went back to talking to patrons. I'd have to deal with my feelings later; I had art to sell.

The show ended, and I walked Cheryl and my dad out and thanked them for coming. Mr. Gaines said that we could talk tomorrow about what people purchased.

"Go home and bask in the success of the opening," he said.

I would do that. I wouldn't let ten minutes of Mike's presence put a damper on what had been a remarkable night. But I didn't lie to myself. I knew there would be no shortage of thoughts about my husband showing up to my show.

CHAPTER 33

SUNNY AND I were having breakfast when Mr. Gaines called to debrief me of the show. While we talked, he sent me an email containing the names of the patrons that had purchased paintings. We had done great, well beyond my expectations. I read quickly through the names thinking that I would send these folks a thank you for their patronage of the arts when my eyes stopped on a very familiar name: Mike Jacobs. He'd purchased the painting of himself. He surprised me showing up and tried to show out on top of all that. It made me feel so sorry that he had been upset. I guess he bought the painting to keep it off display in the gallery, but I was already planning to have it removed.

The doorbell rang. I looked up not expecting anyone. I put Sunny in her playpen and went to the door. When I looked through the peephole, I saw the last face I expected to see there. I opened the door.

"Hey, Mona. How are you?"

Oh, so this was how we are going to do it. Pretend that nothing had happened.

"I'm fine today considering all that happened last night. What are you doing here Mike?"

"Yeah," he said. "About that... that's why I'm stopping by. Mona, I just wanted to talk to you and apologize I guess. I didn't think through what I would say when I was driving over here."

I stepped back from the door so that he could come in. I didn't need a repeat of last night's drama for my neighbors to post on social media. He walked in and stood there. I guess he was waiting on me to make a move, respecting that he didn't live there anymore. I walked past him and back into the kitchen to where Sunny was. Maybe this wasn't the best place to discuss things, but I needed to keep an eye on my baby.

I cleared my throat, "Well, I hadn't expected you to come to the show as you know. Let me apologize first. I shouldn't have included that painting of you in my show without your permission. I'm so sorry I did that... and I'm sorry that you had to see everything on display the way you did. I never expected you to be there."

I picked Sunny up out of the playpen as she started to whine to get out. When I put her on the floor, she instantly crawled to the one cabinet that didn't have a kid lock on and started pulling pot tops out of the rack. I let her do it since this would keep her occupied for a while. Mike looked down at her. I expected to see a look of hatred on his face. It only seemed like he was curious.

"This is the thing Mona; it's not that I'm mad that you had a painting of me in the show. It's just that when I saw our drama on display for everyone to see I got mad as hell. I apologize for showing my ass at the show. I shouldn't have come, but when I heard about the show, I wanted to see what was up."

I sat down at the kitchen table. He continued to stand. We hadn't stood in this kitchen together in months. It felt strange. All those times in the past that he traveled I missed him. Lately, I felt different. I missed him in the way that you missed someone that had passed away. I had banished him out of my life.

"Mike, what did you expect to see?"

He shrugged his shoulders. "I honestly don't know. I thought maybe some flowers or paintings of animals and landscapes or something. What I walked into was a gallery of lies and pictures of our wrecked life. I didn't expect to feel so humiliated like you were punking me in front of all those people. You disrespected me all over again."

Those words hit me like a hard slap in the face. I'd never thought about it like that.

"It wasn't meant to disrespect you. Those paintings were a purging for me. I never dreamed they would be in a gallery. When the opportunity came up for me to follow a passion, I couldn't turn it down. If it makes you feel any better, remember it was my life on display there too. People had no clue what the paintings were about. They simply enjoy the art."

Gallery of Lies

He finally came over to sit in the chair across from me. We used to sit at this table and share meals when times were good. I remembered the last time we sat here. I had been angry and felt self-righteous. It all seemed petty now.

"Why did you do it, Mona?"

"I told you, the gallery owner gave me an opportunity to follow my passion... "

"Nah Mona, that's not what I'm talking about. Why did you cheat on me? But maybe it's the same answer-- you were following your passion."

What do I say? How do I start? We had never had a real conversation about this.

"Come on Mike. Do you want to get into this now?"

Sunny started banging the pot tops together like symbols and laughing like this was the best toy ever. Then she stopped and crawled over to play with a stuffed elephant.

Mike looked startled like he had forgotten she was there. A baby in the house was different for him.

"I do want to talk about this Mona. We should have talked about it a long time ago."

"I tried talking to you, but you didn't want to hear it."

"I know, I wasn't ready then. Now I am."

"I don't even know how to answer now. The reasons that seemed valid to me then feel petty and stupid now. What can I say? You were never here, and I was lonely. But you know all of this."

"Keep going. Tell me," he said.

"I felt isolated and so angry with you that I thought I was justified to have somebody else. I should have been woman enough to separate from you first. I knew better, we both know that infidelity devastated my family. I fell into that common trap of making excuses for myself."

Mike looked down at his hands clasped together on the table.

He said, "You know that I never cheated on you, and I guess I was so complacent that I thought you would never cheat on me either. I thought you would never leave me. I liked the travel. I liked being away. The unhappier you were with me, the easier it was to stay gone. We didn't have kids, so when I found out about Jordan, it felt like I had a chance to be a dad. I was excited about that."

"But why didn't you tell me about it, about him?"

"I don't know Mona. It felt like I couldn't tell you about it. I thought it would be more arguments. I know you would have been mad about who his mother was, but that wasn't an excuse. I also thought you would be upset about me taking even more time away to go and be with him, so I used work as an excuse. Then after a while, I had waited too long to tell you, and it felt impossible."

I could hear car doors opening and closing outside the house. He stood up and walked to the window and looked out for a long time before continuing.

"I was so caught up that I didn't see any of the signs that you were seeing someone else. Well, that's a lie. I noticed that it seemed like you stopped caring that I was gone, but I ignored it."

"If it means anything to you, Mike, I'm truly sorry for the mistakes that I made in our relationship. I'm sorry for the part that I played in fucking up our marriage. I never imagined in my darkest nightmares that we would be separated."

He came and sat back down and put his hand on top of mine on the table. I didn't pull away.

"And I'm sorry for the part I played in fucking up our marriage too. I took you for granted and now look at us. I hated you for months. I still feel some kind of way about it, but I don't hate you anymore. It ate at me so much that I couldn't function at first after I moved out. I had to let all of that go. We are probably past the point of no return, but I miss you. I love you. That hasn't changed. But, I can let go of some of the anger now and live my life, I guess."

He still loved me? I looked at those freckles on his face that I used to count. Before I could think of how to respond, he turned and looked down. Sunny tugged on his pant leg trying to pull herself up as she did with her grandpa.

"Oh let me get her." I stood up, but Mike stopped me.

"She's ok." He reached down and let her grab on to his hand to stand on her chubby legs. She did a little baby jig then fell on her cushioned bottom before crawling over to me.

"She's a handful isn't she?" He stared at her, looking at her face. Then he stood up. "I'm glad we talked Mona."

"Me too," was all I could think to say. Emotions and thoughts raced through my mind.

With Sunny on my hip, I walked him to the front door. He walked out and looked back at me one more time before getting in the car. I closed the door after him. I missed him, and I still loved him too. Too bad we couldn't go back and change things. I looked at my daughter and realized I was thankful that there was a bright spot out of this whole mess.

CHAPTER 34

WHEN I GOT OFF from work, I picked Sunny up from daycare and stopped by CVS to pick up dad's medicine so that I could drop it by his house. I got Sunny out of her car seat and knocked on the door, but he didn't answer it. His car was in the driveway, so I knew he was in there. I hadn't felt like digging for my key with Sunny on my hip, but I did a balancing act, dug it out, and used it to go inside. He wasn't in the front of the house, but when we walked back towards the bathroom, I heard his deep, gruff voice singing some song I didn't recognize. Was he singing in the shower now? Sunny and I settled back into the living room and waited for the water to shut off before I called him to let him know I was in the house. I sat down on the love seat and looked over at that damn raggedy ass recliner. One day I was going to come in here and move that thing out while he was at the barber shop.

Dad finally came into the den a little while later in his white undershirt holding two other shirts on hangers.

"Hey, Monie baby. How are you doing?" I stood up, and he gave me a hug and gave Sunny a big noisy kiss on the cheek that made her giggle.

"Hey, my beautiful grandbaby. What are y'all doing over here?"

"I picked up your medicine to save you a trip."

He rolled his eyes. "I was gonna go by there and get that medicine. I told you I don't need you babying me, but that's ok because I got to see my Sunny today."

I caught a whiff of aftershave. I felt my eyebrow go up in question.

"Dad, where are you getting ready to go? Why do you have on cologne and stuff?"

"Is it too much? This that stuff you gave me as a Christmas gift a while back. I had never opened the bottle, but I think it smells ok."

"Well, yeah dad it smells good... but where are you going?"

Then he held the two shirts up. "What do you think about these shirts? Which one? I like the blue one, but this green one was in the back of my closet?"

He held one shirt up and then the other one. Sunny made a squealing noise.

"I think she likes the blue one. I agree the blue one is better. Give that green one to Goodwill... but you still haven't answered my question."

"Since you insist on being nosy, I will have you know that I'm going to meet a friend in about an hour, so I'm trying to get myself together."

"What friend you going to meet wearing cologne? Mr. Richard doesn't care if you smell good. What are y'all going to do, go play spades or something?"

He slipped the blue shirt on and turned his back to me while he buttoned it up. He was too dark skinned to see a blush on his face, but that was definitely a small smile on his lips.

"Dad! Are you trying to tell me you're going to meet some woman?"

"I'm not trying to tell you nothing, Mona."

"Oh my gosh dad! You are going to meet a woman!" I looked at Sunny. "Sunny do you hear that? Grandpop is going to see a woman. He thinks he is looking fly too."

He laughed his deep rumble of a laugh. "You know I used to be a damn good looking man back in the day. I can still do a little sumthin' sumthin' if I need to."

"Whoa, ok dad. I don't want to hear about all that and what you can do now. So what's the lucky lady's name?"

"Val."

I sucked in air.

"Wait... who? My friend Val? When did all this happen? I saw you two talking at the gallery but how did you hook up?"

Dad walked over to the coat closet and pulled out his gray wool coat that he usually wore to church. He also pulled a black hat with a blue feather from the top shelf. He donned both and turned for me to see.

"How do I look?"

"You look very nice, Dad."

He brushed at the leg of his navy blue slacks and blue button down shirt. He even wore the black lace-up shoes that I had bought him for Christmas last year.

"When we were at the opening, we talked and had some good conversation about you among other things. Val is a very pretty lady, and I know she was checking me out at that birthday party at her house."

I snorted with laughter.

"Yeah, she is pretty dad, but I don't know about her checking you out. But you never want to talk to any of the ladies that try to holla at you at church."

"I never noticed any of them like I noticed Val in that red dress she had on. Then before she left, she asked me for my phone number and I gave it to her. I didn't think we would talk, but we have talked every day since then. Then I asked if she wanted to meet at Paschal's for supper and she said yes."

I patted my dad's shoulder. "Well, that's great, dad. Val is a sweet person with a positive spirit. And Sunny likes her."

At the mention of her name, Sunny giggled.

Dad kissed her on the cheek again. "Yeah, a lot of things happened at that art show. I saw you talking to Mike, and I thought I was going to have to step in and put my hands on him before he left. That wasn't the place to be acting up. I know he's upset about some things, but that wasn't the right thing to do or the right place to do it."

"You're right, but he felt awful because he came by the house the day after and apologized."

It was my dad's turn to raise an eyebrow. "You let him in?"

"I did, and we had a pretty good talk I think. No raised voices."

Dad smirked. "Ok then. That's good. I know he's been having a hard time since you put him out the house. No need to stay mad about things. All it does is eat up your insides. That goes for you too Mona. You have to move on from all of this bad stuff."

I kissed my dad on the cheek. "I know daddy. It's getting better every day. Sunny and I are about to head on out so you can meet Val, I don't want you to keep her waiting. Tell her I said hello, and have fun. Oh, and your medicine is right there on the kitchen counter, please take it like you are supposed to."

"I see that darn medicine over there. I will make sure I take it. Y'all be careful getting home."

"And you text me after you get home from your date, ok?"

"I will. I love y'all."

I walked out and put Sunny in the car seat. My dad was going on a date with a real live woman. About damn time somebody started to find some happiness around here.

CHAPTER 35

WHY HAD I AGREED to meet for sushi? I didn't need no damn sushi. I sat in the car and contemplated going back to the house. I can go by and pick up Sunny from dad's house where he and Val had agreed to watch her while they had a movie night. I could let them get to their Netflix and chill while I took Sunny home and got in the bed with my pajamas and head scarf. I had started to back out of the space when the navy blue pickup truck pulled into the spot next to mine. Could I act like I didn't see him? The midnight black tinted window rolled down, and the face behind it looked at me with a raised eyebrow.

I paused in my retreat and rolled my passenger window down.

"Where are you going Mona? Were you leaving?"

"Ummm, yeah I was. This meetup is a terrible idea, and I've kinda changed my mind about it."

"Come on now Mona. Don't be like that, let's go in and sit down. If you still feel like that after a few minutes, you can leave. You're acting like we're strangers or something."

It sure as hell felt like we were strangers. I pulled back into the parking space and sat there for a minute before getting out of the car. Mike walked around to open my door, but I opened it before he reached it. I fumbled getting my keys out of the ignition and then when I stood up I dropped them on the pavement. He picked them up and handed them to me. I was acting silly then, I knew, but I couldn't help it. He held the door open for me, and we walked into the restaurant. It wasn't crowded, but it was early for dinner, only 5:30. The inside of the restaurant was painted in dark colors of blues and grays with none of the tacky Japanese decor these types of sushi restaurants usually displayed. This place donned more of a modern minimalist approach. The buffet was set up along a bar area in front of the door and another low table to the right of the door. The hostess led us to a table with a little greeting and put down silverware, glasses of iced water, and wooden chopsticks in case you wanted to eat sushi the more traditional way.

After filling our plates with a variety of sushi and other sides we sat there and looked at each other as we both used chopsticks to put the food in our mouths. My hand shook, and I eventually switched to using a fork.

"Mona, why are you so nervous?"

"I don't know. It's like we just met or something."

"It shouldn't be. Just relax. You look good by the way. I like your hair straight like that."

"Thanks. You look nice too."

It looked like he had just gotten a fresh haircut and he wore a simple black t-shirt. He looked good in black. We made small talk and time passed as we got into an old groove of conversation, talking about all the things going on in our lives. We had been living on different planets for the last few months.

"So how's the baby?"

"Oh, she's great. You saw when you came over before how she was pulling up. In a month, I think she'll be walking. I'm biased, but she's a very smart and thankfully, happy baby. At times I didn't know how I would handle everything, but she helped me through it. She gave me a purpose."

He smiled along with me.

"Yeah, I didn't know how much a child could change your perspective on things."

Silence came after that.

"Look, Mona, I don't know what to do or what the right thing is to say. All I know how to do is to say what is in my heart. I've thought a lot about how I should be mad at you forever and how it looks for a man to want to be with the woman that stepped out on him. What would my family, my uncles, or my friends think?"

"Mike please don't explain. I know I humiliated you and there's no getting past that. I understand."

"But Mona what I'm questioning is... is this the end all be all? What is the right way to feel? How do you feel?"

"I try not to think too hard about my feelings anymore. I think about Sunny and her feelings and being the best mom I can be. If I give myself hope for anything else right now, it's just going to be that much harder to keep myself out of the pit that I've been working hard to climb out of. I've struggled, Mike. It was hard to get myself to feel like a normal person that deserved to breathe."

He reached across the table and put his hand on top of mine. I let it rest there and enjoyed the warmth of his palm before I pulled it away, pretending I needed to pick up my glass of water.

We left the restaurant after I made sure that I paid my half of the bill. Across the plaza stood a small bar with a green and white sign over the door that read "Lucky's." There looked to be a few people in there by the number of the cars out front. Mike grabbed my hand and pulled me towards it.

"Let's go have a drink. It's still early."

I thought of Sunny first and then relaxed. She was in good hands. I let him drag me across the parking lot, and when we entered the bar, they played some of that watered down pop music that most people don't notice in the background. A sprinkling of folks in there gave the appearance that this was an after work spot. A blonde, thin-faced woman, sat at the bar with a busty brunette. They both held shot glasses up to toast and then downed the shots with giggly laughter. I briefly wondered how many shots they'd had. A pool table stood in the back, and four guys in khakis and button-down shirts shot a game. We took a seat at the far end of the bar, and Mike ordered my favorite drink before I could protest. The bartender sat the margarita down in front of me, and Mike drank his Hennessey. We looked at people and made up stories of their lives like we used to back in the day. If someone looked at us, I wondered what kind of story they would make up about us. We probably looked like a typical, semi-happily married couple.

Mike sat close to me on the bar stool, his thigh touching mine. He spoke in my ear and put his hand on the small of my back as he did. It was comfortable and familiar. The drinks made me warm, so I stopped at two and asked the bartender to add more juice to the second one that I didn't finish. I hadn't drunk much alcohol since I'd given birth, and it wasn't a good time to overdo it.

Walking back to the car Mike held my hand, and when he opened my door, I let him embrace me. We stayed hugged up for longer than we needed to. Even after all we had been through, the core of me was still drawn to this man. If I wasn't mistaken, I could feel that he was still drawn to me too. He kissed me on the cheek then pecked me on the lips in that dry way platonic friends kissed. Then something drove me to kiss him again. I pressed my lips to his, and my body shaped itself to his tall form.

I thought I would have time to talk myself out of letting Mike come back to the house on the drive home, but the bar was only ten minutes from the house. We walked to the front door like a couple of teenagers trying to find a place to make out after the prom. Inside the foyer, clothes slid off and buttons broke. We landed in our marriage bed; our limbs wrapped up together. I looked at the freckles in my husband's face once again as he moved over me looking down into my eyes. He slid inside of me, and it felt the way it had ten years ago when we couldn't get enough of each other. In those times, we didn't need food or water and survived off lovemaking for days at a time. That was before he traveled, and I got lonely.

I woke up at the ringing of my phone and saw a picture of my dad's face on my screen.

"Oh shit, I have to go get Sunny."

Mike's hand wrapped around my waist and pulled me even closer. I wanted to savor this moment, I wanted to lay there and wish tomorrow wouldn't come too soon, but I had to get up. I answered the phone.

"Hey, dad. I'm sorry. I'm on my way now."

"Hey, Monie it's ok. I'm just checking in. It's only 8:19. Are you alright?"

I looked at the clock. It seemed so much later than that.

"Yeah, yes, dad. I'm fine. I'm headed over there to get Sunny. She's not giving you trouble is she?"

"Naw, she's already in her pajamas laying here asleep on the love seat. Don't rush. It's Friday, enjoy yourself."

"Ok, dad. I will see you in a few minutes."

Mike raised his head.

"Everything ok?"

"Yeah, it is, but I need to get up. We fell asleep, and I have to go and get Sunny."

He pulled me closer and kissed the side of my neck.

"I know you need to go. I didn't intend to fall asleep either," he laughed. "I didn't intend any of this, but I'm glad it happened."

I didn't respond. *Was I glad?*

I extricated myself from the bed. Mike looked at me. He knew me. He knew I was having doubts. I wanted to know what all this meant. Now wasn't the time to have a therapy session. Taking my cue, he didn't press me to stay but got up and went into the bathroom. It felt like old times like home was supposed to feel. I went into the guest bathroom, washed up, and slipped on some yoga pants and a t-shirt. There was no need of putting my clothes back on. Dad might question it, but he was a smart man, he probably wouldn't ask anyway.

I walked with Mike to the door. He hugged me again and kissed me on the lips the same way he used to when he was leaving to go on one of his trips. Only this time instead of me wishing for him not to go, it felt like he was coming home.

CHAPTER 36

AT THE BREAK OF DAWN, the next morning my phone chimed while I was in the bathroom doing my hair, getting myself ready for work. I picked it up to see a text.

> Hubby: Good morning Mona. I enjoyed yesterday. Let's get together again.

I stood there with the phone in my hand typing and deleting words until a glance at the clock let me know I was going to be late to work if I didn't hurry my ass up. I finally responded

> Me: Good morning. Enjoyed it too. Have a good day.

I didn't want to commit to any more dates with Mike. I wasn't sure that I wanted to continue down this path of reconciliation. It would take a lot of hard work that may still eventually end in us being apart. Why go through that heartbreak again?

The next day and every day after that I got a text from Mike asking me how I was doing. The texts then turned to daily phone calls. He asked about Sunny. He asked about dad and my work day. He let me know what was going on with his life. We kept the conversation pretty light, not delving into the hard stuff.

He usually called me early in the morning before work. We stayed on the phone for no more than five minutes and made small talk. I started to look forward to the daily calls to start my day. One night though, he called me after

I had put Sunny down to sleep. He said he'd been to Charlotte for a few weeks and stayed with his mom.

"I hadn't told her about my son either. When I told her, she lit into me for hiding it. She was mad and accused me of keeping her one and only grandchild from her."

It made sense. I always felt that Mike's mother resented me for not producing a baby early in our marriage.

"She just started back talking to me after two weeks. She asked me about you."

I murmured, "I'm sure she had a lot to say about me."

"She probably didn't say what you think she would. Of course, she had a lot to say about you when I told we separated, but mom has changed a whole lot over the years. She used to be so stern and mean when I was a kid. Do you remember that time we didn't visit her for Thanksgiving, she didn't talk to me for damn near seven months?" He chuckled, "I think losing my dad, and then my uncle has made her more forgiving. You know she and her brother hadn't talked for years before he died. She regrets that. I don't want to have that kind of regret Mona."

I didn't have anything to say to that. I had enough regret for both of us and three other people, but it looked like we could be on the road to overcoming any bitterness between us.

***

Cheryl invited me to her house for Sunday brunch.

"Yeah, girl it seems as if I am dating my husband," I said. "You know I told you about that first time we went out, and we ended up doing it. I was unsure about what to do after that. But he started texting and calling me every morning. You know I have always been a sucker for those early morning greetings."

Cheryl put a pitcher of mimosa on the table and sat down. I busied myself pouring syrup over the golden brown Belgian waffle on the white plate in front of me. She also served up some thick slices of bacon and some sort of cheesy egg quiche type of thing. Cheryl could do her thing in the kitchen.

"So what else has he been doing besides texting you? I know there has to be more to it than that?"

"Well, it started the week after that date with him offering to come by and bring dinner for Sunny and me. He brought me some Mexican food and even thought enough to bring Sunny a banana. He had me wondering where he had gotten advice on what babies liked to eat."

I poured mimosa in my champagne glass and took a gulp. It was delicious. It tasted like it had a hint of mango in it.

"Then we went out to a movie and to see some live jazz performance at that little seafood bistro over there in Edgewood. We have been doing things that we haven't done since before we were married. He even took me up to the spot where we used to go and park and make out so long ago."

Cheryl took a sip of her mimosa and looked at me with pursed lips.

"Yeah, Mona, that's cool, but get to the nitty-gritty. Have you been sexing each other like crazy every time you get together or what?"

I looked down and took a big bite of bacon and eggs and waffle. I chewed and swallowed and took another sip and concentrated on cutting my waffle to take another bite.

"Mona, don't play. You ain't that interested in your food. Stop shoveling food in your mouth and give me the details."

I couldn't do anything but laugh before giving in.

"Girl, we haven't had sex every time, but it's been a few more times. It's like this is the exact relationship that I wanted with my husband before our marriage went all to hell. We are spending time together. I don't let him come around too much with Sunny there though. I don't want her to get used to him being around."

"Yeah, I can understand that. But how do you handle that? Does that come up in conversation?"

"We don't talk about it too much. I know it's the elephant in the room. We don't discuss anything that happened, and I don't want to bring it up because I'm so busy enjoying all this attention. I know it's not realistic to think it's going to continue to go this smoothly if we don't address our problems. One time when we were together, Mike mentioned something about trying to go to counseling. I kinda just glazed over it all and changed the subject."

Cheryl dipped a spoon into one the sweet parfaits that she had served as a dessert.

"Girl, it may be worth it to go to counseling for your marriage even if it's just to get closure for it. You said that talking to that psychologist helped you with your postpartum issues. It can't hurt."

Yeah, but counseling is also very painful when you start digging up all of the bad feelings and painful memories. I don't know if I'm ready to go through all that with Mike right now.

Cheryl leveled me with a sober look. "So Mona, as your oldest friend I'm going to ask you. What is it that you do want? What are you ready for? Let's be real here; it has been a rough year for your ass. You almost died in an accident. The man that you had a relationship with died. Your husband found out you were cheating and left you, but now it seems like he is trying to become a part of your life again. There's no such thing as storybook ending, but maybe your marriage will survive."

I flinched at having my life summarized in a few short sentences that hit me like stones. "You don't have to be so blunt Cheryl."

She reached across the table and grabbed my hand. "I wasn't trying to be mean or hurt you with what I said, but we always said we would call each other on bullshit and be real with each other when it's needed. I'm just saying, it's probably time for a reality check and for you to decide what you genuinely want to do with your marriage. If you want out of it, now is the time to make that decision before you and Mike get back in it too deep. Neither one of you could stand the hurt again."

"You don't think I know that? I'm just enjoying my little bubble of happiness right now. Stop trying to burst it. Can I ignore reality for a few more weeks, damn? I can't stand your '*always gotta be pointing out stuff and being realistic and trying to help me better my life*' ass."

We both burst into a fit of high pitched giggles that only true girlfriends could understand.

"Believe me, Cheryl, I think about this every day. I reflect on the days when I got involved in that affair, and I wonder what was missing to make me get out there and do what I did. I think it was insecurity and loneliness and stupidity. That was the bottom line. I should have just separated from Mike or done something to let him know how unhappy I was with the situation. Hell, we both had to be unhappy because he kept things from me as well. I don't know where our friendship broke down to where we stopped being honest with each other. Now, it's like he's the perfect husband. But I'm skeptical though. How long can this last? Will we revert to the old unhappy couple? I don't know."

"Girl after the way the communication has broken down between Ray and me, all I have to say is my opinion is that you should try to work things out with Mike. He is a good guy, and there's not a whole lot out there. I now understand being lonely in a way that I never did before. When people say they are alone in their marriage, I completely get it now. I was on your side before Mona when you used to complain about Mike's absence, but I'd never experienced those feelings. Ray's been MIA."

It was my turn to console and give advice. "Cheryl, you and that man have a long history, and I know you two love each other. All I can say is you have to fight for it. You can't just sit back and play the blame game about who is doing what to whom. That will get you nowhere. Maybe if y'all can go to counseling you can get to the root of why he's acting like this. But don't let it go. Keep trying to talk to him. And leave the pride out of it. You are going to have to make yourself vulnerable."

She swiped a hand across her face before jumping up suddenly to start clearing the dishes from the table. When her back was to me, I saw her try to swipe a hand across her face discreetly. My friend did not cry. I stood up and walked over to her.

"Cheryl, I think you're going to have to let your husband see this when you try to talk to him. You are a hard nut to crack. Men's egos can't take that all the time. Let him see you break down. Show him that you're hurting. I think it could help."

She turned and hugged me. I started tearing up too. How did we end up this way? We sat down and finished the bottle of champagne while we switched the topic to gossip around the office and laughed about the latest happenings on reality TV. We were both strong Black women, but when things fell apart, we had to show each other how strong we could be and help each other to heal.

CHAPTER 37

CHERYL SAT IN MY visitor chair like usual, munching on a grilled chicken salad with lemon juice we had ordered online from the deli on the corner. She frowned as she chewed and looked at my calzone with disdain.

"I can't believe you are just going to sit there and eat that right in front of my face. Look at all that cheese."

I lifted a chunk of the calzone to my mouth, and a string of mozzarella cheese trailed back down to the plate. I took a bite and closed my eyes in abandon. Cheryl chewed her bite of salad more vigorously.

"Hateful bitch," she said under her breath.

"Girl, you could've ordered the calzone; that was your choice."

She stood up and tugged at her black pencil skirt.

"Do you see this? This is from all them damn chips I've been eating and wine I've been drinking. I almost needed pliers to get this zipper up this morning."

She sat back down, and I laughed. We talked more office gossip as we finished our lunches when Cheryl's phone rang.

"It's Ray. I'll be back."

She got up from the chair and stepped out into the hallway walking towards her office. I turned around to my computer and tapped back into the report that I was supposed to finish by Friday. Just as I clicked on the spreadsheet, Cheryl ran back into my office and closed the door.

"Mona, Ray says he's being arrested. I have to go. I don't know what I need to do. I'm not going to tell them where I'm going. If anybody asks, can you tell them that I got sick?"

I jumped up out of my chair.

"What? Why is he being arrested? Do you want me to come with you?"

She turned, and the fear on her face was real.

"No, no. Both of us can't leave suddenly. I'll call you when I find out what's going on."

With that, she turned and walked out of my office. I stood there and watched as she snatched her bag and keys out of the desk drawer and jogged in her high heels towards the side exit.

I trashed the remnants or our lunches and tried to get back to work on the report, but the numbers on the screen ran together. It was futile to pretend I could do any work at that point. I searched the internet to kill time and looked at social media. After an hour, I decided it was a waste of energy to continue to sit at the desk doing nothing. I still hadn't heard from Cheryl and when I called her phone went to voicemail. I decided to go on home.

At home, I changed out of my wrap dress and blazer and donned a pair of leggings, and an old stretched out North Carolina Tar Heels sweatshirt. I clicked on the television when a channel two Action News breaking story banner popped up on the screen. My hand flew to my mouth. I immediately tried to call Cheryl again. I texted Mike and told him to turn on the news. I couldn't believe what I was seeing. Ray's Auto Shop had been raided.

***

The chirping of the cell phone pulled me out of a dream that I couldn't remember. I hit the side button to silence the ringer, slid out of bed, and stepped out of the bedroom before answering. I didn't want to wake Sunny.

"Cheryl girl, what happened? I saw the news, and I have been waiting on you to call me back."

Cheryl's voice sounded raspy. She had been crying.

"Yeah, I've been up at the police station and the courthouse. I couldn't get back to you. I tried to bail Ray out, but he will be in there overnight. I got him a lawyer, trying to see what the bail will be."

"Girl, the news said he was part of an illegal gambling ring. I know that has to be a mistake."

Cheryl sobbed into the phone.

"Mona, I don't want to say anything yet. I'm still trying to figure out what is going on. He isn't saying much right now, I will find out more tomorrow. Just pray for him and pray for me. I'm scared of what I'm going to find out tomorrow when I get to the bottom of this whole mess."

CHAPTER 38

"I CAN'T BELIEVE Ray got caught up like that though. When I saw him on the news, I was so shocked. He never said anything to me," Mike said as he ran a hand over his face.

"Well, he didn't say anything to anybody. Cheryl didn't have a clue. Evidently some guy he used to run with back in the day convinced him that they'd never get caught. Cheryl said he told her he needed the money to save the shop, so he let the guy put those illegal slot machines in that empty suite for a piece of the profits. That explains the Camaro he bought. I guess he got a big payout."

"I just hope this doesn't ruin them," Mike said.

After those words, we both got quiet, probably thinking about what had ruined us. I didn't want to think of what would happen if Ray went to trial. My friend would be devastated.

Saxophone notes glided through the air smelling of dusk and honeysuckle. We sat on the tailgate of his truck looking out over the city. It was just like old times except now the truck was newer, and we'd made too many mistakes. Our thighs touched while we sat there swaying to the music. Dinner had been good, and I kept to my pledge of one glass of wine. I didn't want to compromise my judgment. I remembered my conversation with Cheryl a month ago and heard her sassy voice in my head telling me to make a choice. Every night I struggled with the type of indecision that I only prayer would help. Some nights my racing thoughts pushed me out of my bed and down on my knees asking for the spirit of discernment.

What-if scenarios clouded my mind. We broke marriage vows, but wasn't it our duty as the people who had taken those vows in the eyes of God to try and make things work out? Mike put his arm around me and pulled me close against him, his big hand stroking up and down my arm. Tonight would lead us to the bedroom again if I didn't do anything to stop it.

He slid off the truck to stand up and pulled me up with him. We slow danced to the music. Then he started to whisper in my ear.

"Mona, I want to move back home."

I stopped mid-step and would have stumbled had it not been for his hand supporting my lower back. I pulled back and looked into his face to see if this was a joke. He held my face in his hands and held my gaze.

"I'm serious Mona. I've done plenty of soul searching about this. I don't know how things are supposed to go or if it's meant for things to work out between us. I don't know anything for sure right now, but we have to try harder, don't we? I want to try. I don't want this to be the end of our relationship because it's not supposed to be that easy to give up. I wanted to..."

I held my hand up. "Mike you don't have to..."

He put a finger up to my lips. "Mona, please listen to me and let me say what I have to say. I wanted to give up. Over this past year, I have hated myself for still caring about you. I tried not to love you anymore. You already know how I felt, we don't have to rehash that. But in the past few months, I realized that I'm not done with us yet. I think we have to try and give it a chance. I want to get to know Sunny, and I want you to meet Jordan."

He dropped his finger from my lips, so I guess that was my cue to respond.

"Mike I admit that I've been thinking about all this. I don't want to get my hopes up. We have a broken trust to repair. The thing I worry about is whether you will be able to accept Sunny. I don't want her to suffer because of some situation that I put her in. I know you won't intentionally mistreat her, but I don't know if I trust that you will fully accept her. And it's the same with your son. I don't know how I will be to accept him fully. I don't know if we can be the Brady Bunch or if that is even a realistic expectation. That's what scares the shit out of me. Instead of it just being two people hurt, it could end up being four people hurt in this situation."

I walked back at forth as I talked. Mike stood still looking at me as I moved around. I'd been trying to avoid this moment. I had to make a decision.

"Mike, I need to think about this some more." I stopped pacing. "I can't say what I want right this second because I don't know what that is. Give me some time to think about it, but I promise that I will have a definitive answer before we see each other again. We don't need to keep getting together without knowing for sure how we are going to play this."

I took his hand in mine. "Do you understand that?"

He smiled at me, and my arms wanted to go around him, kiss him, make love to him and forget all of this.

"Yes, I do understand baby. I didn't expect you to say I could move in tonight, but I had to let you know what I want."

I released his hand. Instead of kissing him, I went over to the passenger side door of the truck and opened it. He walked around and closed the tailgate and by the time he opened his door I was sitting inside, buckling my seatbelt. He got in and buckled his. The jazz music still played, its sweet melodies floating inside the cab of the pickup. He cranked the truck and put it in gear. Before he pulled off, he looked over at me.

"Whatever you decide Mona, just know that I love you."

"I love you too."

With that, he drove me home.

***

The next day, when I pulled up to his house, dad stood there watering his grass. As soon as Sunny recognized our location, she started laughing and chanting in her high pitched voice, "Gwanpop, gwanpop, gwanpop!"

Dad smiled and put the hose down.

"Now look-a-here, if it ain't two of my favorite ladies."

I couldn't get Sunny out of the car seat fast enough. I put her down, and she waddled over to him as quickly as her little inexperienced legs would let her. Dad picked her up, and Sunny smacked the side of his face with her lips. I went to him and gave him a smack on the other cheek.

He laughed, "Lawd knows I didn't do nothing to deserve all of this here loving. Y'all come on in the house. I just got some p-o-p-s-c-i-c-l-e-s. Can she have one?"

"Dad that little girl is so smart she probably knows what you're spelling. But yeah, she can have one. I'm going to have one myself."

We got inside, and I almost tripped on the carpet from shock.

"Dad! Where's your recliner?"

He smiled wide. "What do you think?"

In place of the recliner sat a brand new sectional sofa with a chair on the end that had the latch on the side for you to recline. The old sofa and loveseat that had been in this room since I could remember was also gone.

"I can't believe it. When did you get this furniture? Oh my! Is that a new rug? This room looks incredible!"

He was full out laughing now. Sunny was already attempting to climb up on the tan cushions but couldn't quite get a good hold to lift herself. I went over and gave her little bottom a boost and then sat down next to her, bouncing like I was a kid myself.

"It's cozy in here now. I can't believe this. I've been trying to get you to get rid of that recliner for ten years."

"There was nothing wrong with my recliner ten years ago. But the other day the arm separated from the side. I had fixed it one time before, but Val was over here when it happened. I was a little embarrassed. Mama raised us to keep our things looking nice and for it to look neat and clean even if we didn't always have money to buy expensive things. I realized I have money in my savings, and there wasn't a reason for me to have that raggedy chair in here. I saw how Val looked at it. She didn't say anything, but she had that look on her face that all you women get when you don't approve of things. So, I asked her to come with me to pick out a set. Well, really, I picked it out because I have good taste, but you know, I asked her opinion here and there."

"Well, well, well. Ok then, dad, I'm just glad that raggedy chair is gone. Thank you, Jesus."

We both laughed together. Sunny was trying to stand up on the sofa now.

"No, no Sunny. We don't want you to mess this up. This couch might be in here another forty years."

Dad shot me a look, and I laughed.

We got Sunny settled in the high chair he had bought to keep over here for her. He even had a stash of bibs that I hadn't purchased. Undoubtedly, that had also been one of Val's touches. Dad and I sat across from each other sucking on popsicles. Just like when I was a little girl, I ate red, and he ate grape. It didn't matter what flavor the red was, I always got red, and I noticed that Sunny preferred the same thing. Neither of us ate the banana flavored ones. Who likes banana popsicles anyway?

"So dad, I want to talk to you about something." He looked at me with a raised eyebrow.

"What is it? This sounds serious."

"Well, it is. I haven't said much to you about it, but I have been going out with Mike pretty regularly."

He smirked, "I hope you don't think I hadn't figured that out already?"

"What? How did you know?"

"I know things. I may not be able to see that good without my glasses, but my vision's good enough to see you've been a little happier. Plus, you've been dropping Sunny off over here to go somewhere."

"That doesn't mean anything; I could have been going on dates with another man."

"Yeah, but I didn't think you would be out there doing that at this point without being divorced. Plus when I talked to Mike, he already let the cat out of the bag. You know how he gets when he's excited about something," he chuckled.

"I should have known. Well anyway, it's been like when we first met. I've enjoyed all the time we've spent together, but now it's time to get out of limbo. Did Mike tell you that he asked to move back in?"

"No, he didn't tell me that, but I figured that was coming. I thought he would have asked before now."

"But dad, what should I do? I don't want to get my hopes up for it all to come crashing down again later."

He finished his last bite of his treat and turned to me.

"Mona baby, I'm not going to sit here and tell you what to do and neither am I going to tell you what you want to hear. I don't know what the right answer is. You are talking to somebody that hasn't been in a relationship in thirty years. When I found out that you had been with that other guy it hurt me to my heart so much. All I kept thinking was that it wasn't going to end right. All I could see was your mama and how it ended for her and us. You made a mistake though, and all human beings do that, but God gave you another chance at life. If there was any way your mama could have survived, all I can say is that I would have forgiven her because that woman was the love of my life. I would've been mad as hell, but I wouldn't have been able to let her go. Hell, after she died, I still didn't let her go. That's why I never had other women around me longer than a few weeks."

I sat up straight in my chair. "Dad, I have never heard you talk about that. It just seemed like you weren't interested in women anymore, not like that."

"I wasn't. I mean I'm still a man, so I was interested in women obviously, but I didn't want one coming around trying to be my wife and all that. I didn't want one coming in trying to be your mother because you had a mother. That's just how I felt. So I never let you meet any of them."

"I guess today is just a day for surprises," I said.

"Mona, what I said probably doesn't help you any, but you have to do what your heart tells you. Don't leave your brain out of the decision, but let the heart drive and your brain can navigate if you get lost. It won't be easy if you two get back together. And if you think Mike won't love my grandbaby like she's his or if you can't accept his son then don't waste your time."

CHAPTER 39

THE TREES IN THE PARK swayed in the breeze dressed in the gold and burnt umber of fall. I sat on a blanket watching Sunny run around on her little fat legs picking up the leaves that had fallen from the trees and exploring everything with the wonder that children viewed the world. She tried to run too fast in one direction and landed on her bottom in a fit of giggles that made me giggle along with her. I got up and chased her around a little while and then checked my phone. They were supposed to be here in about five minutes. I looked down the hill towards the playground and then over near the parking lot. I didn't see them yet. I sat back down on the blanket to take a sip of water when I saw them walk over the hill. There was Mike's tall form that I recognized, and next to him a bit shorter figure walked with his shoulders a bit hunched.

I held Sonny's hand, and we both stood there and watched them get close to us. When they stopped, Mike put his hand on the boy's shoulder.

"So Mona, this is my son Jordan. Jordan, this is my... this is Mona."

Here stood a younger, thinner, carbon copy of Mike down to the freckles sprinkled on his tan cheeks. There was no denying this boy was Mike's son. I stuck out a hand, and he shook it tentatively. Sunny ran over to Mike and pulled on his pant leg and spoke to him in baby gibberish. It almost sounded like she was telling him off. He reached down and picked her up and swung her up in the air. I felt the nervousness start to melt away. Jordan looked at me, and I asked him a few questions about school and hobbies. He had good manners. I could tell his mother had taught him well.

We left the park and went for ice cream. Mike mentioned a new video game and Jordan perked up then. He had been nervous as well. By the time I arrived back home and pulled Sonny's sleeping form from her car seat, I had made a decision.

***

We arrived at the counselor's office building, and it looked nothing like I expected. I rechecked the address and confirmed that the purple building was the location of McMillan Family Counseling. I looked over at Mike, but he didn't return my gaze. He just opened his car door, and I heard a long sigh escape from him. I didn't blame him; I was apprehensive about this too. We didn't talk about things and let others into our business, but I was willing to try this if it would help.

When we entered the office is when I realized that I had not known what to expect. My experience with counseling was through video chat. I supposed I thought there would be a chaise lounge where we would be forced to lie back while the doctor hypnotized us into telling our deepest and darkest secrets. A soothing shade of sage green covered the walls. Burgundy drapes hung from the windows and in the center of the room sat a huge mahogany desk flanked by a beautiful set of bookshelves filled with books and photographs. Over to the right stood a grouping of overstuffed chairs in an antique gold color facing a large overstuffed dark wine leather couch. Over to the left, there was an area that held a colorful rug with train tracks on it and a few toys and books on a low shelf. We were alone in the office until a door that I had not noticed opened from the far left and a short brown-skinned woman entered the room.

I had talked to Dr. McMillan on the phone when I made the appointment, and she looked like she sounded. She had a deep rich voice that would be perfect for radio. She had her graying short dreadlocks pulled back with a red scarf tied around them. She wore a long full black skirt with a white shirt topped by a red blazer. Boots with four-inch heels encased her feet which meant her true height had to be only about five feet tall. She clasped first my hand and then Mike's before motioning for us to take a seat.

"Do you want us to sit on the sofa?"

She smiled and said, "Wherever you would like and where you will feel the most comfortable."

We looked at each other and sat on the big couch. The doctor didn't say anything; she just waited for us to take our seats and settled in one of the chairs. This office looked nothing like I pictured it.

"Well, let me start by introducing myself. I'm Dr. Vanessa McMillan. You may call me Vanessa, Dr. McMillan, or whichever makes you feel the most comfortable. What I specialize in is marriage and family counseling for African- Americans. Let me warn you that I am very upfront and honest in my assessments. I don't always believe that a couple needs to stay together, but I do try to help people make their relationships healthier and more functional when there is love there. I won't sugarcoat anything, and the best way for you to get anything out of this is to be completely honest in here. If you can't be completely honest at this point, then there is no need to move forward with counseling. Now, tell me why you're here."

I didn't know why, but I already liked Dr. McMillan. Her last statement terrified me, but I started the conversation.

"I'm Mona. I talked to you on the phone. We've been married for eleven years, and a lot of bad things have happened that we're trying to move past. We're here to save our marriage."

She sat back on the couch.

"Ok, Mona." She looked over at Mike who looked at me as I talked. "Now what about you, do you have anything to add?"

Mike looked at her. "I'm Mike, and I'm here because I think we can move forward. Mona suggested we come here. I'm not sure I believe talking to a stranger can help, but I'm willing to give this a shot."

"The good thing is that you agreed to come. That was a huge first step. Now I'm going to start with you, Mona. Why don't you tell me everything that you want me to know about your marriage for the past ten years, kind of a synopsis if you will."

What I told her didn't take long. I explained how we met. I expressed my feelings about Mike's traveling and then I told her about my affair.

The session drained me. I knew the benefits of therapy, so I trusted the process, but it was still hard to listen to Mike describe the pain I caused him.

The next day, Mike moved back in, and after almost a year, I slept in our master bedroom with my husband.

CHAPTER 40

MR. GAINES MET ME at the back door of the gallery, the salt overtaking the little bit of pepper he still had remaining in his hair. He gave me a firm hug, and big smile that always took over his face when he saw me. Our partnership had become a lucrative one for both of us. Later in the month, we would discuss the prospect of me taking over the gallery and allowing him to retire to travel with his wife.

He put his arm out, I linked my arm through his, and we walked through the storage room to the front of the gallery.

"Everything is in place. Do you remember how nervous you were before your first show? You're a pro at this now though aren't you?"

I thought back to the fits of nerves that had ruled me the night of that first show. I laughed to myself about the amount of time I'd spent just trying to find an outfit to wear. The white pantsuit I chose for tonight was classy and comfortable. I had twisted a royal blue scarf around my neck to complement the suit and the theme of the show.

"Mr. Gaines, it's all because of you. I'm so glad you wanted to host my first exhibition."

"I recognized your talent. I'm fortunate that you took me up on my offer. If not, I wouldn't have been able to groom someone to run this gallery. I hope you take me up on this new venture. I know you're the perfect person to run this place. You have such a good eye. My wife is ready for me to retire so we can finally get to do all this traveling she's been bugging me about for years."

I patted his hand as we walked.

"I told you that I'm still thinking about it."

I never thought that my career would be so fully immersed in this art world. Running a gallery and having the responsibility of curating quality pieces scared me. It was overwhelming to think I wouldn't have Mr. Gaines's input every day.

"Mona, you just have to trust your gut. You've soaked up everything that I could possibly teach you in these four years, and I think you're ready. I believe in you. Don't let the fear stop you. Come on, give an old man a break."

I could only laugh. I thought I had made up my mind, but I didn't want to say anything yet.

The gallery space was pristine white, but this time I had added a royal blue treatment to the floor. The name of the show, Closing Doors, was stenciled in cursive letters throughout the space. Once the team and I put every item in place to the minutest detail, the show started and I finally relaxed. The apprehension I felt with my first gallery opening was long gone. These paintings would hold no surprises for anyone. Jazz music played over the speakers as people picked up flutes of champagne and sparkling water from the wait staff trays. I mixed and mingled and answered questions about my inspiration and what the paintings meant. Being contrite with my answers was tempting. I flung statements around like, "It means what you want it to mean." Or "It's not about the artist, it's about how it makes you feel." I had learned that the patrons just wanted to hear a story and make a connection. I understood that now. I started painting to tell my story when it felt like all of my connections had been severed.

This time around I could look at most of the paintings and associate them with a happy memory. I looked at the one of my dad in his tux dancing with Val in her ivory lace dress. I hoped that I had captured the joy on both of their faces in their first dance as man and wife. This show included another picture of Cheryl, this time with Ray cupping her face as he gazed into her eyes. It had almost broken Cheryl when the judge sentenced him to jail; but when he got out after eleven months for good behavior, they realized they couldn't live without each other. On the opposite wall hung a picture of Sunny, holding her paint brushes, imitating mommy. I couldn't believe she was in school now, talking the teachers' heads off.

"So who are the people in the painting?"

I knew the question was coming but didn't think I would be so emotional talking about it for this show. I should be an old pro at this now.

I turned and stared at the painting the couple referred to. The blurred and abstracted image still easily discernible to see the figures. The browns, golds, and oranges of fall surrounded the shapes. Specks of color represented the leaves in the park. The silhouettes looked to walk side by side. What the viewer saw was a family. A man with his arm around a woman's shoulders as she held the hand of a little girl. Holding the little girl's other hand as she walked in her pink dress was another male figure, slightly shorter and slimmer than the other male figure in the painting. This male appeared to be a boy, perhaps a teenager the viewer may conclude.

The short-haired woman that asked the question looked at me expectantly.

I spoke, "It's a family that I used to know."

The man with her spoke up, ignoring my answer.

"Gina, it's easy to see this is a family. It reminds me so much of us. This is exceptional work, I love this one. It would look good in the family room wouldn't it, over the sofa?"

I took it that Gina was his wife, and she forgot all about me once they started to discuss how the colors would bring out the orange in their rug and the red in the curtains. I eased away from their conversation about the happy family painting that would add to the happiness of their household. When I had finished that painting three years ago, it hung in my own dining room. In a house that had seen so much. When I had put it there, we overflowed with hope and the promise of forgiveness and new beginnings. I was in love with my husband all over again, and Sunny had gained a father after losing one that she had never known. I had gained a son, a tall and awkward mild-mannered boy whose face mirrored his father's freckles.

That painting had stayed there until I had decided to put it in this show with the hopes that someone would see the happiness there and buy it. I didn't want to hang it in my new place. That was for new beginnings, wasn't it? I was happy to put a 'SOLD' sticker next to that painting for the couple before the night was over. Hopefully, I had gained a loyal customer who would purchase my art. Hopefully, they got a painting that they could enjoy in their home.

Sunday morning I woke to the sun shining on my face super early. I couldn't help it, the kids always got me up early and out of bed. But this morning the first thing on my agenda was to call Mr. Gaines to tell him to go ahead and set up the meeting. I had decided as I drove home from the show last night. I was ready to take this next step in my life. He was so excited when I told him the news. His wife even got on the phone to thank me. I got up, dressed, pulled my wild hair up into a bun, and put on a pair of Yoga pants to get some work done around the house before Mike got here.

A little after three, the doorbell rang. I put the chicken in the oven and went to the door. When I opened it, Sunny stood there waiting to give me a big hug, and I reached down to give her a kiss. Mike slammed the car door and walked towards the door.

"Mommy, daddy took me and Gracie to get ice cream today."

I smiled at my firstborn. "Is that right?"

Mike held a sleeping Gracie in his arms. I let him walk in and closed the door behind him. He carried her to her room and then came back into the living room speaking to Sunny.

"Daddy's going to be back to pick you up in two weeks, and we're going to the zoo ok"

Sunny looked at me smiling, "Can mommy come to the zoo with us?"

Mike stood up and looked me in the eye. "Mommy is welcome to come if she wants to, but she may be busy."

"Sunny, baby go play on your iPad for a little while until it's time for dinner."

Mike smiled, "So, mommy, are you coming to the zoo with us?"

I smirked, "I just might. You never know. It has been so long since I have been down to that zoo. I went back when Willie B was still alive. So how is Jordan? Has he gotten the hang of driving yet?"

Mike smacked his teeth. "That boy thinks he can drive, but every time I get into the car with him, I feel like I'm hurtling to my death. He will be alright. It's just that the Atlanta traffic terrifies me. How are you settling in?" he asked.

I looked around the room. "It's good; I like it. I still have boxes to unpack, but I like the space. I'm glad the other house sold so quickly."

With a slight smile he said, "Yeah, me too. Just to let you know, Gracie did alright sleeping through the night this time. I think she's getting used to my condo."

After that, we made a few more minutes of small talk, and my mind flashed back to the gallery and the painting of the family that couple bought. That life had lasted for a little while. Gracie had been a surprise to both of us, but Mike was a good father to both of the girls. We just couldn't make it work. But we could say that we had tried hard. He would always be a part of my life now, and I still loved him as the father of my children.

In the painting I sold, it portrayed a happy family: a husband, a wife, a little girl and a son walking hand in hand.

Mike had walked out the front door and headed back to his truck when I called out to him.

"Hey, is Jordan planning to go to the zoo with y'all?"

He turned to answer. "Yeah, he's actually excited to take the girls. He's been telling Sunny about the giraffes and lions. I know he can't wait for her to see it in person."

I shrugged a shoulder. "You know what? I am going to come with y'all if that's alright."

He laughed, "Of course, it's alright Mona."

We could go to the zoo and still look like the figures in that painting. Who's to say that we hadn't found our version of a happy family?

THE END

ABOUT THE AUTHOR

Lolah Howard has been writing stories since she was in elementary school. An engineer by trade, Lolah spent the last decade writing her debut novel, Gallery of Lies. She lives in Atlanta, GA. Visit her on the web at www.lolahhoward.com.

Made in the USA
Columbia, SC
10 September 2019